Selection and Translation

Anthony Ramírez

The Best of

LATIN AMERICAN SHORT-STORIES

─────────────

Los
Mejores **CUENTOS**
HISPANOAMERICANOS

First Series - Primera Serie

❖

BILINGUAL BOOK PRESS

FIRST EDITION - 1994

The Best of

LATIN AMERICAN SHORT-STORIES

———

Los
Mejores **CUENTOS**

HISPANOAMERICANOS

Selection and Translation:
Anthony Ramírez

First Series - Primera Serie

BILINGUAL BOOK PRESS
Quality Bilingual Publications

THE BEST OF LATIN AMERICAN SHORT STORIES

Series director: Bernard H. Hamel

Published in the United States of America
by Bilingual Book Press, 10977 Santa Monica Blvd.,
Los Angeles, CA 90025.

ISBN 1-886835-02-0

To my parents, Antonio and Aurora León Ramírez; as well as, José and Antonia Gonzales, my godparents, in memoriam.

Also to an outstanding family, dear friends and without question the finest physicians in California: Drs. Fred, Robert and Bill Horowitz.

TABLE OF CONTENTS

INTRODUCTION

The reader will find these stories to be different and truly varied in content. A reflection, to be sure, of the vast "riqueza" of literature to be found in Hispanic letters.

Further still, *The Best of Latin American Short Stories* is of particular value to teachers and professors of Spanish who are looking for new and exciting material to enhance the study of the language. And, especially so for librarians in our so-called "knowledge and information society" who find themselves thrust, more and more, in the role of teacher and instructor of research skills; notwithstanding their usual perceived responsibility for knowing and introducing literature; plus fostering an appreciation of culture and reading. The latter, an endeavor that will be made that much easier since these stories are attention holding, filled with fantasy, feeling and symbolism.

Students today –and people tend to overlook this fact– are much more attuned to the graphic and visual. What appears to be a lack of interest in the scholastic, particularly with respect to reading and the written word, is perhaps nothing more than an unstated request or demand for better and higher quality written material; stories that are real, meaningful, lively or moving. Sometimes we tend to place the blame on "them", but could it not also be that WE should cultivate a new mindset in both how we work and teach the new generation? Is instruction and information the same thing? Perhaps we need to explore new methods of presenting each of these, so that our work and the materials which we share, ultimately, really do capture and hold the attention of still another generation brought up -not just on television- but on television and computers, computer games and videos.

Much is said today about the "global world" and the changes taking place in society. And, without question, technology is im-

portant, since it links the planet as never before. However, to be truly effective in this new world environment, one must possess something else that machinery alone cannot provide: intercultural awareness and understanding. I call it cultural literacy; someone else, and I prefer this definition, refers to it as "cultural protocol".

This, then, should not be viewed as just another collection of short stories in translation. Far from it! This text helps introduce the reader to the various cultures represented. And, indeed, one will learn much to increase cultural literacy, by reading the "cultural cues" contained in these stories.

Learning is now ongoing and this material will help the individual enhance his knowledge of Latin American cultures. As such, it is providing an understanding of culture, and, therefore, empowering the student, manager and team-worker of the future. For one of the greatest skills to possess, so the experts say, includes not just specialized or advanced training, nor command of another language, but an *understanding* of how to work with diverse groups of people all over the world; and –why not say it– with the diversity of groups that live right here in our own country.

Could it be that Hispanic letters, albeit in translation, may help revive a greater interest in reading? These stories are both interesting and highly descriptive; therein, in fact, lies their strength. They stimulate the reader's imagination. Are there other stories? To be sure, the electronic links being put into place today will enable us to discover and access a plethora of such material.

This is truly an exciting time. An era of reorganization and reinvention in both industry and education! More importantly it is a time for realization that in the world of education –like the world of business– there are no borders.

A. Ramirez
Oxnard, California, 1994

Horacio Quiroga
Uruguay (1878-1937)

Horacio Quiroga's stories fall into three general categories: stories for children *(Cuentos de la selva)*, stories which reflect an early influence of the works of Edgar Allen Poe *(La gallina degollada, y otros cuentos)*, and most characteristically stories which depict man's struggle against the forces of nature at its violent worse, usually taking place in the most unfriendly areas such as the jungle region of Uruguay and Argentina. These locations, however, were of the writer's own choosing. Quiroga, much in the manner of Hemingway, felt that before he could truly write, he needed to live a fuller life in order for his writing to thrive. The ever-recurring drama of life and death and survival in the open wilderness was the daily bread that kindled his spirit and sustained his writing. He could never be the aesthetic, intellectual writer characterized by the literary schools of the day; but one that conveyed the vital, dynamic pulse of life in its primitive environment.

The story chosen for the present selection reflects the lighter (although no less intense) side of the writer's personality. Life is a struggle to be sure, but there are happy moments, as in the case of becoming the happy father of two small children. Laughter and joy and the warmth of companionship and the intimacy of family life, not entirely devoid of mischief, pervade this story.

EL LORO PELADO

Por Horacio Quiroga

Había una vez una bandada de loros que vivían en el monte. De mañana temprano iban a comer choclos a la chacra, y de tarde comían naranjas. Hacían un gran barullo con sus gritos, y tenían siempre un loro de centinela en los árboles más altos, para ver si venía alguien.

Los loros son dañinos como la langosta, porque abren los choclos para picotearlos, y después se pudren con la lluvia. Y como al mismo tiempo los loros son ricos para comer guisados, los peones los cazan a tiros.

Un día, un hombre bajó de un tiro a un loro centinela, el que cayó herido y peleó un buen rato antes de dejarse agarrar. El peón lo llevó a la casa, para los hijos del patrón, y los chicos lo curaron, porque no tenía más que una ala rota. El loro se curó muy bien, y se amansó completamente. Se llamaba Pedrito. Aprendió a dar la pata; le gustaba estar en el hombro de las personas y con el pico les hacía cosquillas en la oreja.

Vivía suelto, y pasaba casi todo el día en los naranjos y eucaliptos del jardín. A las cuatro o cinco de la tarde, que era la hora en que tomaban el té en la casa, el loro entraba también en el comedor, y se subía con el pico y las patas por el mantel, a comer pan mojado en leche. Tenía locura por el té con leche.

Tanto se daba Pedrito con los chicos, y tantas cosas les decían las criaturas, que el loro aprendió a hablar. Decía: "¡buen día, lorito...!" "¡rica, la papa...!" "¡papa para Pedrito...!" Decía otras cosas

THE PARROT WHO LOST ITS FEATHERS

By Horacio Quiroga

Once upon a time there was a flock of parrots that lived in a woodland. In the early morning they would go and eat sweet corn cobs at a farm, and in the afternoon they would eat oranges. They made quite a fuss with all their noisemaking, and always had a parrot as a lookout in the tallest trees, to see if someone was coming.

Parrots are as destructive as locust because they open sweet corn cobs to peck at them and then these spoil with the rain. But at the same time since parrots taste so good cooked as stew, the farmhands would hunt and shoot them down.

One day, someone with one shot, fell a parrot lookout, who came crashing down from the injury and put up a good fight before letting himself be caught. The farmhand took it to the master's children at the house, and the youngsters nursed it back to health, since the only thing wrong with him was a broken wing. The parrot healed quite well, and became altogether tame. They called him Pedrito. He learned how to offer his leg as if to shake hands; he enjoyed being on people's shoulders and with his beak would tickle a person's ear.

He went about freely, and would spend most of the day in the orange and eucalyptus trees in the garden. At four or five o'clock in the afternoon, which was the accustomed time for tea at the house, the parrot would also go into the dining room, and with his beak and feet would climb up the tablecloth and eat bread moistened with milk. Indeed, he was absolutely mad about tea with milk.

Pedrito shared so much time with the youngsters and they said so many things to him, that the parrot learned how to speak. He could say: "Good day, little parrot...!" "Delicious food...!" "Food for Pedrito...!"

13

más que no se pueden decir, porque los loros como los chicos, aprenden con facilidad malas palabras.

Cuando llovía, Pedrito se encrespaba y se contaba a sí mismo una porción de cosas, muy bajito. Cuando el tiempo se componía, volaba entonces gritando como un loco.

Era, como se ve, un loro bien feliz, que además de ser libre, como lo desean todos los pájaros, tenía también, como las personas ricas, su "five o'clock tea".

Ahora bien, en medio de esta felicidad, sucedió que una tarde de lluvia salió por fin el sol después de cinco días de temporal, y Pedrito se puso a gritar volando:

–¡Qué lindo día, lorito...! rica, papa...! ¡la pata, Pedrito...! Y volaba lejos, hasta que vio debajo del él, muy abajo, el río Paraná, que parecía una lejana y ancha cinta blanca. Y siguió, siguió volando, hasta que se asentó por fin en un árbol a descansar.

Y he aquí que de pronto vio brillar en el suelo, a través de las ramas, dos luces verdes, como enormes bichos de luz.

–¿Qué será? –se dijo el loro–, Rica papa...!" ¿qué será eso...? "¡buen día Pedrito...!"

El loro hablaba siempre así, como todos los loros, mezclando las palabras sin ton ni son, y a veces costaba entenderlo. Y como era muy curioso, fue bajando de rama en rama, hasta acercarse. Entonces vio que aquellas dos luces eran los ojos de un tigre que estaba agachado, mirándolo fijamente.

Pero Pedrito estaba tan contento con el lindo día, que no tuvo ningún miedo.

–¡Buen día, tigre! –le dijo– "¡la pata, Pedrito...!"

Y el tigre, con esa voz terriblemente ronca que tiene, le respondió:

–¡Bu-en dí-a!

–¡Buen día!, tigre! –repitió el loro–. "¡Rica, papa...! ¡rica papa...! ¡rica papa...¡"

Y decía tantas veces "¡rica papa!" porque ya eran las cuatro de la tarde, y tenía muchas ganas de tomar té con leche. El loro se había olvidado de que los bichos del monte no toman té con leche, y por esto lo convidó al tigre.

–¡Rico, té con leche! –le dijo–. "¡Buen día, Pedrito...!" ¿Quie-

He was also able to say other things one should not repeat, because parrots, like children, learn naughty words with the greatest of ease.

When it rained, Pedrito would get upset and talk to himself, saying all sorts of things, in a very low voice. But when the weather got better, he would then fly around and scream like crazy.

He was, as you can see, a very happy parrot, that besides being free, as all birds wish to be, also had, like rich people, his "five o'clock tea".

This notwithstanding, in the midst of all this happiness, it so happened that on one rainy afternoon the sun came out at last after five days of stormy weather, and Pedrito began to fly and scream.

"Pretty day, little parrot...! Yummy, food...! Pedrito, shake my finger ...!" And he flew quite a distance, until he saw below him, far below him, the Paraná river, which looked like a wide and distant white ribbon. Still he continued, on he flew until he finally alighted on a tree to rest.

And it so happened that all of a sudden he saw on the ground, through the foliage, what appeared to be two green lights, like enormous fireflies.

"What is that?" the parrot said to himself. "Yummy, food...!" "What can that be...?" "Good day, Pedrito...!"

The parrot always spoke that way, just like all parrots do, mixing words without rhyme or reason, and at times it was difficult to understand him. And since he was very curious, he started coming down branch by branch, till he got close. It was then that he saw that these two lights were the eyes of a tiger that was crouched down, staring at him.

But Pedrito was so happy with the beautiful day, that he wasn't at all afraid.

"Good day, tiger!" he said to him– "Pedrito, shake my finger...!"

And the tiger, with that terribly raucous voice of his, answered:

"Go-od day!"

"Good day, tiger!" replied the parrot.

"Tasty, food...! Tasty, food...! Tasty food...!"

And he kept on saying "Tasty, food!" because it was already four o'clock in the afternoon and he was very anxious to have his tea with milk. The parrot, however, had forgotten that the animals of the woodland don't drink tea with milk, so he invited the tiger to join him in having some.

"Tasty, tea with milk! "he said to him. "Good day, Pedrito...! "

res tomar té con leche conmigo, amigo tigre?

Pero el tigre se puso furioso porque creyó que el loro se reía de él; y además, como a su vez tenía hambre, se quiso comer al pájaro hablador. Así es que le contestó:

—¡Bueno! Acérca-te un po-co, que soy sor-do!

El tigre no era sordo; lo que quería es que Pedrito se acercara mucho para agarrarlo de una zarpazo. Pero el loro no pensaba sino en el gusto que tendría en la casa cuando él se presentara a tomar té con leche con aquel maravilloso amigo. Y voló hasta otra rama más cerca del suelo.

—¡Rica, papa, en casa! —repitió, gritando cuando podía.

—¡Más cer-ca! ¡No te oigo! —respondió el tigre con su voz ronca.

El loro se acercó un poco más y dijo:

—¡Rico, té con leche!

—¡Más cer-ca toda-vía! repitió el tigre.

El pobre loro se acercó más aún, y en ese momento el tigre dio un terrible salto, tan alto como una casa, y alcanzó con la punta de las uñas a Pedrito. No alcanzó a matarlo, pero le arrancó todas las plumas del lomo, y la cola entera. No le quedó una sola pluma en la cola.

—¡Toma! rugió el tigre—. Anda a tomar té con leche...

El loro, gritando de dolor, se fue volando. Pero no podía volar bien, porque le faltaba la cola, que es como el timón de los pájaros. Volaba cayéndose en el aire de un lado para otro, y todos los pájaros que lo encontraban, se alejaban asustados de aquel bicho raro.

Por fin pudo llegar a casa, y lo primero que hizo fue mirarse en el espejo de la cocinera. ¡Pobre Pedrito! Era el pájaro más raro y más feo que puede darse, todo pelado, todo rabón, y temblando de frío. ¿Cómo iba a presentarse en el comedor, con esa figura? Voló entonces hasta el hueco que había en el tronco de un eucalipto y que era como una cueva, y se escondió en el fondo, tiritando de frío y de vergüenza.

Pero entre tanto, en el comedor todos extrañaban su ausencia.

—¿Dónde estará Pedrito? —decían—. Y llamaban: —¡Pedrito! ¡Rica, papa, Pedrito! ¡Té con leche, Pedrito!

"Do you want to drink tea and milk with me, my good tiger friend?"

But the tiger became furious because he thought that the parrot was making fun of him; and what's more, since he too was hungry, he decided he wanted to eat the talkative bird. So he answered him in the following way:

"Good! Get a little clo-ser, I'm hard-of-hearing!"

The tiger of course was not hard of hearing; what he wanted was for Pedrito to get much closer so he could grab and catch him. But the parrot was only thinking about the pleasure it would give him to show up to have tea and milk with such a magnificent friend, and he flew to still another branch closer to the ground.

"Yummy, food, at home!" –he repeated, at the top of his voice.

"Get clo-ser! I can't hear you!" replied the tiger with his raucous voice.

The parrot got just a little bit closer and said:

"Tasty, tea with milk."

"Still even closer!" repeated the tiger.

The poor parrot got closer still, and at that moment the tiger gave a terrific leap, as high as a house, and with the tip of his nails, caught hold of Pedrito. He wasn't able to kill him, but he pulled out all the feathers from his back, and those of the entire tail. Not one single feather remained on his tail.

"There!" –roared the tiger– "Now you can go and have your tea with milk..."

The parrot, shrieking with pain and fear, took off flying. But he couldn't fly very well, since he was missing his tail which in birds serves as a rudder. He could fly but he kept falling in the air from one side to the other, and every bird that met him, would distance themselves frightened by the sight of this strange animal.

Finally he managed to get home, and the first thing he did was to go and look at himself in the cook's mirror. Poor Pedrito! He was the strangest and ugliest looking bird you could ever imagine, entirely without feathers, without a tail, and trembling from the cold. How was he going to show up in the dining room, in such a shape? He then flew into the hollow of the trunk of a eucalyptus tree which was like a cave, and hid at the back of it, shivering from both the cold and embarrassment.

But meanwhile, in the dining room everyone missed him.

"Where can Pedrito be?" they were saying. And they would call out: "Pedrito, delicious food, Pedrito! Tea with milk, Pedrito!"

Pero Pedrito no se movía de su cueva, ni respondía nada, mudo y quieto. Lo buscaron por todas partes, pero el loro no apareció. Todos creyeron entonces que Pedrito había muerto, y los chicos se echaron a llorar.

Todas las tardes, a la hora del té, se acordaban siempre del loro, y recordaban también cuánto le gustaba comer pan mojado en té con leche. ¡Pobre Pedrito! Nunca más lo verían porque había muerto.

Pero Pedrito no había muerto, sino que continuaba en su cueva sin dejarse ver por nadie, porque sentía mucha vergüenza de verse pelado como un ratón. De noche bajaba a comer, y subía en seguida. De madrugada descendía de nuevo, muy ligero, e iba a mirarse en el espejo de la cocinera, siempre muy triste porque las plumas tardaban mucho en crecer.

Hasta que por fin un día, o una tarde, la familia sentada a la mesa a la hora del té, vio entrar a Pedrito muy tranquillo, balanceándose, como si nada hubiera pasado. Todos se querían morir de gusto cuando lo vieron, bien vivo y con lindísimas plumas.

—¡Pedrito, lorito —le decían—. ¡Qué te pasó, Pedrito! ¡Qué plumas brillantes que tiene el lorito!

Pero no sabían que eran plumas nuevas, y Pedrito, muy serio, no decía tampoco una palabra. No hacía sino comer pan mojado en té con leche. Pero lo que era hablar, ni una sola palabra.

Por esto el dueño de la casa se sorprendió mucho cuando a la mañana siguiente el loro fue volando a pararse en su hombro, charlando como un loro. En dos minutos le contó lo que le había pasado; su paseo a Paraguay, su encuentro con el tigre, y lo demás; y concluía cada cuento, cantando:

—¡Ni una pluma en la cola de Pedrito! ¡Ni una pluma ¡Ni una pluma!

Y lo invitó a cazar al tigre entre los dos.

El dueño de la casa, que precisamente iba en este momento a comprar una piel de tigre que le hacía falta para la estufa, quedó muy contento de poderla tener gratis. Y volviendo a entrar en la casa para tomar la escopeta, emprendió junto con Pedrito el viaje a Paraguay. Convinieron en que cuando Pedrito viera el tigre, lo distraería charlando, para que el hombre pudiera acercarse despacio

But Pedrito did not move from his cave, nor did he answer, remaining silent and motionless. They looked for him everywhere, but the parrot did not show up. So everyone thought that Pedrito had died, and the youngsters began to cry.

Every afternoon, at tea time, they would always remember the parrot, and recall how he enjoyed eating bread moistened with tea and milk. Poor Pedrito! They would never see him again because to them he had died.

But Pedrito had not really died, instead he remained hidden in his cave not allowing himself to be seen by anyone, because he felt a great deal of embarrassment seeing himself as bare as a mouse. At night he would come down to eat, and go back up right away. At dawn he descended again, in somewhat of a rush and would look at himself in the cook's mirror, still quite sad however because the feathers were taking a long time to grow back.

Until at last one day, or rather one afternoon, the family, seated at the table at tea time, saw the parrot come in quite untroubled, moving about to and fro, as if nothing had happened. They were all overjoyed with happiness when they saw him, very much alive and with extremely beautiful feathers.

"Pedrito, little parrot!" they said to him–. "What happened to you, Pedrito? What colorful feathers the little parrot has!"

But they did not know that these were new feathers, and Pedrito, in quite a serious fashion, was not about to say anything. He just kept eating bread moistened with tea and milk. But as far as speaking, not a single word.

This is why the owner of the house was greatly surprised when on the following morning the parrot flew onto his shoulder, talking just like a parrot. In a couple of minutes he told him what had happened. His trip to Paraguay, his encounter with the tiger, and so on; and he would end every story singing:

"Not one feather on Pedrito's tail! Not one feather! Not one feather!"

And he invited him to go and hunt the tiger between the two of them.

The owner of the house who it just so happened was about to buy a tiger skin which he needed as a rug for his pot-bellied stove, looked forward to getting one free. And after returning to his house to get his gun, he set out together with Pedrito on the trip to Paraguay. They both agreed that whenever Pedrito would see the tiger, he would divert his attention with his conversation, so that the man could gradually get

con la escopeta.

Y así pasó. El loro, sentado en una rama del árbol, charlaba y charlaba, mirando al mismo tiempo a todos lados, para ver si veía el tigre. Y por fin sintió un ruido de ramas partidas, y vio de repente debajo del árbol dos luces verdes fijas en él; eran los ojos del tigre.

Entonces el loro se puso a gritar:

—¡Lindo día...! ¡rica papa...! ¡rico té con leche...! ¿quieres té con leche...?

El tigre enojadísimo al reconocer a aquel loro pelado que él creía haber muerto, y que tenía otra vez lindísimas plumas, juró que esta vez no se le escaparía, y de sus ojos brotaron dos rayos de ira cuando respondió con su voz ronca:

—Acércate más! ¡Soy sor-do!

El loro voló a otra rama más próxima, siempre charlando:

—¡Rico, pan con leche...! ¡ESTÁ AL PIE DE ESTE ÁRBOL...!

Al oír estas últimas palabras, el tigre lanzó un rugido y se levantó de un salto.

—¿Con quién estás hablando? —bramó—. —¿A quién le has dicho que estoy al pie de este árbol?

—¡A nadie, a nadie! —gritó el loro—. —Buen día, Pedrito... ¡La pata, lorito! Y seguía charlando y saltando de rama en rama, y acercándose. Pero él había dicho: Está al pie del árbol para avisarle al hombre, que se iba arrimando bien agachado y con la escopeta al hombro.

Y llegó un momento en que el loro no pudo acercarse más, porque si no caía en la boca del tigre, y entonces gritó:

—¡Rica, papa...! ¡ATENCIÓN!

—¡Más cer-ca aún! —rugió el tigre, agachándose para saltar.

—¡Rico té con leche...! ¡CUIDADO, VA A SALTAR!

Y el tigre saltó en efecto. Dio un enorme salto, que el loro evitó lanzándose al mismo tiempo como una flecha en el aire. Pero también en este mismo instante el hombre, que tenía el cañón de la escopeta recostado contra un tronco para hacer bien la puntería, apretó el gatillo, y nueve balines del tamaño de un garbanzo cada uno, entraron en el corazón del tigre, que lanzando un bramido que

closer with the shotgun.

And that's exactly what happened. The parrot, seated on the branch of a tree, talked and talked aimlessly, while looking all around for a glimpse of the tiger. Finally he heard the noise of parting foliage, and all of a sudden saw under the tree two green lights looking straight at him; they were the eyes of the tiger.

Then the parrot started to shriek:

"Beautiful day...! Delicious, food...! Tasty tea with milk...! You want tea with milk?"

The tiger, upon recognizing that featherless parrot, which he thought he had killed, and which once again had beautiful feathers, became furious and swore that this time the parrot would not get away, and a wrathful look flashed from both his eyes as he replied with his raspy sounding voice.

"Come just a lit-tle clo-ser! I am hard of hear-ing!"

The parrot then flew to another branch slightly closer, chatting all the while:

"Tasty, bread with milk...! HE'S AT THE FOOT OF THE TREE...!"

Upon hearing these words, the tiger let forth a tremendous roar and jumped up.

"Who are you talking to?" he howled. "Who have you told that I am at the foot of this tree?"

"No one, no one" shouted the parrot. "Good day, Pedrito... Shake my finger, little parrot!" And he kept on chatting and jumping from branch to branch, and getting closer. But he had said: "he's at the foot of the tree" in order to warn the man, who crouched all the way down and with his shotgun on his shoulders was getting closer and closer.

There came a time when the parrot could not get any closer, because if he did so he would fall right into the tiger's mouth, and at that moment he shouted:

"Tasty, food...! CAREFUL!"

"Still clo-ser yet!" roared the tiger, crouching down in order to jump.

"Tasty, tea with milk...! BE CAREFUL, HE'S GOING TO JUMP!"

And the tiger did, indeed, jump. He gave an enormous leap, which the parrot avoided by hurling himself at the same time like an arrow into the air. But at the same instant the man, who had the barrel of the shotgun leaning against the trunk of a tree in order to aim better, pulled the trigger and nine pellets, each the size of a garbanzo bean, entered like a flash into the heart of the tiger, which letting forth a

hizo temblar el monte entero, cayó muerto.

Pero el loro, qué gritos de alegría daba! Estaba loco de contento, porque se había vengado —¡y bien vengado!— del feísimo animal que le había sacado las plumas.

El hombre estaba también muy contento, porque matar a un tigre es cosa difícil, y además tenía una piel para la estufa del comedor.

Cuando llegaron a la casa, todos supieron porque Pedrito había estado tanto tiempo en el hueco del árbol, y todos lo felicitaron por la hazaña que había hecho.

Vivieron en adelante muy contentos. Pero el loro no se olvidaba de lo que había hecho el tigre, y todas las tardes, cuando entraba en el comedor para tomar el té se acercaba siempre a la piel del tigre, tendida delante de la estufa, y lo invitaba a tomar te con leche.

—¡Rica, papa...! —le decía— ¿Quiere té con leche...? ¡La papa para el tigre! Y todos se morían de risa. Y Pedrito también.

❖

great roar that made the entire woodland shake, fell dead.

But the parrot, who was shouting with joy, was utterly happy, because he had avenged himself –and well avenged at that– from that terribly ugly animal that had plucked his feathers.

The man was also very pleased, because to kill a tiger is not an easy thing to do, and besides he now had a tiger skin as a rug for the dining-room's pot-bellied stove.

When they arrived at the house, all learned why Pedrito had spent so much time in the hollow of the tree, and everyone congratulated him for the feat he had just accomplished.

From then on they lived very happily. But the parrot could not forget what the tiger had done to him, and every afternoon, upon entering the dining room to take tea he would always go to the tiger skin, spread out in front of the pot-bellied stove, and invite him to take tea with milk.

"Tasty, food...!" he would say to it. "Want tea with milk...? Food for the tiger!" And everyone would break into laughter, including Pedrito.

❖

María Silva Ossa
(Chile)

This charming story about a boy and
the unique experience related in this
story will undoubtedly bring to the
reader's mind Jonathan Swift's renowned work: *Gulliver's Travels.* Indeed there are various similarities.
The use of fantasy as a means of re-
flecting on human nature and society, embodying that which is ideal in
the unreal and by contrast exposing
the vicissitudes of the real world.
While Cervantes accomplished the
same objective by turning Don
Quijote into a madman (to be sure,
such an idealist cannot be real), Swift
choose to accomplish this by way of
fantasy. This technique is success-
fully employed by the Chilean writer
to weave an entertaining and exem-
plary story of a young boy on the
threshold of adulthood.

EL BARCO DE MAS ALLA

Por María Silva Ossa

Alejo, sentado a la orilla del mar, contemplaba las olas plácidas que se deslizaban hasta casi tocarlas. Le adormecían los reflejos multicolores de las aguas, cuando un extraño objeto lo despertó completamente. ¿Estaría soñando? Una gran botella con un barquito dentro cayó de golpe en la arena. Alejo corrió a recogerla. El barco en miniatura era realmente perfecto. Trató en vano de sacarlo de la botella; el cuello de ésta se estrechaba más y más. Tampoco podía quebrarla, no tenía fuerza para ello.

De repente creyó oír un leve movimiento en el barco. "Quizá –pensó– alguna arenilla que ha caído dentro". Pero al mirar con fijeza, notó a un grupo de hombrecillos minúsculos que caminaban por la cubierta del barquito y lo señalaban a él, con los brazos extendidos.

Muerto de miedo, soltó la botella, que al golpear una roca se rompió con estrépito. Por suerte el barco no sufrió daño alguno; antes bien, quedó encajado en la arena con su arboladura intacta.

Los hombres gesticulaban todos a un mismo tiempo. Alejo, no sabía si retirarse o llevar el mágico juguete para su casa. Optó por lo último. Con mucho cuidado alzó el barquichuelo y caminó apresurado hacia la casa.

–¿No hay nadie más aquí? –preguntó a la empleada que abrió la puerta.

Al saber que sus padres estaban ausentes, entró en la sala de baño y, llenando la bañera, colocó el barco en el agua. Las velas se

26

THE SHIP FROM FAR WAY
By María Silva Ossa

Alejo, seated at the edge of the sea, was contemplating the placid waves that spilled forth almost within reach. The multicolored reflections of the water were about to lull him to sleep, when a strange object fully awakened him. Could he be dreaming? A large bottle with a little ship inside fell with a thud on the sand.

Alejo ran to pick it up. The miniature ship was perfect in every detail. He tried in vain to take it out of the bottle; but its neck, however, kept getting narrower and narrower. Nor was he able to break it, not having the strength to do it.

Suddenly he thought he heard a slight movement in the boat. "Due perhaps" –he thought– "to a little bit of sand which may have fallen inside". But upon taking a closer look, he noticed a group of tiny little men walking along the deck of the small boat and they were pointing to him with extended arms.

Frightened to death, he let go of the bottle, which upon hitting a rock broke with a crash. Luckily the boat did not suffer any damage; on the contrary, it became stuck in the sand with its masts and spars intact.

The men were all gesturing at the same time. Alejo did not know whether to leave it there or to take the magical toy to his home. He opted for the latter. With a great deal of care he lifted the tiny little ship and walked hurriedly towards home.

"Is there no one else here?" –he asked the maid who opened the door.

Upon learning that his parents were not at home, he went into the bathroom and, filling the bathtub, placed the ship in the water.

27

desplegaron y los hombrecitos corrieron por la cubierta, desapareciendo luego en el interior de la nave. Alejo no se atrevió a dejar sola su joya y, sacando el buque del agua, lo escondió debajo de su cama.

Por fin llegó el momento de acostarse. Luego de rezar se disponía a dormir, cuando un ruido de voces le hizo dar un salto; los marineros uno a uno abandonaban la nave y trepaban con agilidad las frazadas. El capitán se plantó delante de Alejo, que lo miraba mudo de espanto.

—¿Hasta cuando vamos a continuar con este jueguito? ¡Sabes perfectamente que no somos juguetes! —susurró lleno de furia.

—Usted parece un juguete —respondió Alejo—. De todos modos no podía dejarlos a ustedes botados en la playa, con un barco tan pequeño.

—¡Tienes que llevarnos inmediatamente hasta el mar! Debemos cumplir una misión difícil. Te recompensaremos si nos ayuda. ¡No te pesará!

Alejo se vistió sigilosamente, tomando todas las precauciones imaginables para que nadie lo viera salir de casa.

Con el barquito entres sus manos, se dirigió al mar. La noche se iluminaba de luna llena. El mar parecía tan tranquillo como una rica sopa de leche. Los hombrecillos se deslizaron fuera de la embarcación, y el capitán explicó al niño:

—Nosotros venimos de muy lejos; las cosas lejanas siempre se ven pequeñas; las botellas con barcos dentro son de más allá. Eres el primer niño que ha tocado lo distante. Y lo distante se aprecia verdaderamente. Por ejemplo, cuando tú esperas la Pascua, estás loco de alegría imaginando la fiesta y los regalos que recibirás; la Pascua llega y dejas de comer muchas de las golosinas que te han regalado; ya no te apetecen tanto. Y los juguetes nuevos pronto dejan de interesarte; prefieres los que tu propia mano fabrica: cajitas, palos, alambres, muñecos de cartón y trapos. Pues nosotros somos aquello que aún no has alcanzado; tus deseos no cumplidos. Podríamos ser juguetes, pero como tenemos vida, no lo somos. No te cansarás con nosotros, porque no te pertenecemos. Quizá si te empequeñecieras navegaríamos durante esta noche de luna llena, y así conocerías la alegría de vivir entre nosotros.

28

The sails unfolded and the little men ran along the deck, soon disappearing inside the ship. Alejo did not dare leave his jewel of a find alone and, taking the vessel out of the water, he hid it underneath his bed.

At last it was time to go to bed. After praying, just as he was getting ready to go to sleep, the sound of voices made him jump; the seamen were abandoning the vessel one by one, and nimbly climbing the blankets. The captain placed himself in front of Alejo, who was looking at him mute with fright.

"How long are we going to go on with this little game? You know perfectly well that we are not toys!" He murmured quite infuriated.

"You look like a toy" –replied Alejo–, "Anyway, I could not leave you stuck out there on the beach with such a tiny ship."

"You must take us immediately to the sea! We have to carry out a very difficult mission. We will reward you if you'll help us. You will not regret it!"

Alejo got dressed discreetly, taking all imaginable precautions so that no one would see him leave the house.

With the little ship in his hands, he headed towards the sea. The night was lit up by a full moon. The sea seemed as tranquil as a bowl of savory milk soup. The little men slid outside of the ship, and the captain explained to the child:

"We come from far away; far off things always appear small: bottles with ships inside of them are from far away. You are the first child to touch that which is distant. And that which is distant is highly esteemed. For example, when waiting for Christmas, you are overjoyed imagining the party and the gifts you will receive; Christmas comes and you refrain from eating many of the sweets that have been given to you; they no longer appeal to you. And the new toys soon cease to interest you as well; you prefer the ones you make yourself: little boxes, sticks, wires, rag and paper dolls. Well, we are that which you still have not attained; your unfulfilled wishes. We could be toys, but since we are alive, we are not. You will not get tired of us, because we do not belong to you. Perhaps, if you were to become tiny we would sail throughout the night under this full moon, and in that way you would discover the joy that it is to live among us."

Alejo, fascinado, respondió que iría con ellos.

El barco levó anclas y el mar con mucho cuidado lo sostuvo sobres sus olas. Qué diferente era lo que contemplaba ahora, a lo que estaba acostumbrado a mirar; sus ojos traspasaban la superficie del mar y distinguían peces y plantas de colores y formas hermosísimos. Los peces lo saludaban, seguros de que Alejo nada les haría, porque el niño sólo sentía la felicidad de tener tantas cosas para sí, sin desear en ningún momento comérselas o destrozarlas.

Por fin arribaron a una isla: la misma que él soñara tantas veces; el pasto tierno era suave, sin espina, ni pedruscos, y los árboles estaban llenos de toda clase de frutas a la vez.

Muchísimos enanitos salieron de sus casas a su encuentro. También eran semejantes a los juguetes que él nunca tuvo. Había carros con ruedas gruesas, molinos, puentes y trencitos de madera pintados de rojo y negro.

Los habitantes de la isla hablaban con voces de flauta. Le hicieron entrar en una casita con techo pintado de acuarela. Varios canarios entonaron una melodía dulcísima. La dueña de casa era igual a la muñeca que su hermana pidió en la última Pascua, y que ya había roto. El no necesitaba tocar los juguetes; le bastaba vivir con ellos y comprenderlos.

—¿Te sirves torta? —preguntó sonriente la dueña de casa.

Alejo, con sólo mirar la torta, sintió su gusto en el paladar y un agradable calorcito en el estómago. De esa manera se hartó de los manjares más ricos, sin tener que abrir la boca para tragarlos.

—Lo bello pertenece a todos —explicó un muñeco viejo, que sentado en un sillón de balancín contemplaba al niño—. Estás dichoso porque no has tenido el deseo de apropiarte de lo que has visto acá; gozas jugando, comiendo sin comer y sintiéndote bueno al no romperlos. Somos la naturaleza. Te pertenecen la tierra, el mar, los caminos. A medida que crezcas, sabrás utilizarnos, pero si tratas de retenernos sufrirás y envejecerás pronto. Goza de las cosas como si en realidad no fueran tuyas sino de todos; en último término, de Dios.

Alejo siguió el consejo del hombrecillo, y durante horas jugó con cuanto pudo, respetándolo todo como si otros también tuvie-

Alejo, fascinated, answered that he would go with them.

The ship set sail and the sea with great care sustained it on its waves. What he now beheld seemed so different from what he was used to seeing; his eyes penetrated the surface of the sea and were able to distinguish fish and plants of extremely beautiful colors and forms. The fish greeted him, certain that Alejo would not harm them, because the boy seemed to be content and satisfied to be able to partake of so many things, without even for a moment desiring to eat or destroy them.

At last they arrived at an island: the same one that he had dreamed of so many times; the tender grass was soft, without thorns, nor rough stones, and the trees were filled with fruits of all kinds.

Several dwarfs came out of their homes to meet them. They were also similar to the toys he never had. There were cars with thick wheels, windmills, bridges and wooden trains painted red and black.

The inhabitants of the island spoke with voices that sounded like flute music. They showed him into a small house with a watercolor painted roof. Various canaries intoned the sweetest melody. The mistress of the house was just like the doll that his sister had asked for last Christmas, and which she had already broken. He did not need to touch the toys; it was enough for him to live with them and understand them.

"Would you like some cake?" asked the lady of the house, smilingly.

Alejo, by simply looking at the cake, sensed its taste in his palate and a pleasant warmth in his stomach. In that way he had his fill of the richest foods, without having to even open his mouth to swallow them.

"Beautiful things belong to all of us" explained an old doll, that seated in a rocking chair was observing the boy–. "You are happy because you have not had the desire to appropriate for yourself some of the things you have seen here; you're able to have a good time, eat without eating and feel good about yourself for not breaking us. We are part of nature. Land, sea and roads belong to you. As you grow up, you will learn how to make use of us, but if you try to keep us you will suffer greatly and age very quickly. Enjoy all things as if in reality they did not belong to you but rather to everyone; or if you wish, to God."

Alejo followed the advice of the little man, and for many hours played with everything that he could, treating all things with care as

ran que jugar después de él.

El velero navegaba sin hundirse nunca; su puente era largo y pulido como un deslizador.

Cuando la luna hizo un guiño, el capitán del barco le dijo que regresara a casa; sus padres sufrirían al no encontrarlo.

Alejo se despidió con gran cariño y, cosa rara, sin tristeza; sabía que los encontraría a cada momento en los diversos lugares del mundo.

Los árboles, el río, los pájaros y sus juguetes serían para él objetos de eterna dicha.

Miró el mar y deseó estar en su casa. Corrió alborozado a contarle a su hermana el viaje maravilloso que había realizado.

—Ahora nunca nos aburriremos —le dijo—, conocí el mundo distante y me he dado cuenta de que lo que deseamos lo tenemos a mano; hay que saber mirar y vivir unidos a las hermosas cosas del mundo.

Y los niños muy felices, comenzaron a jugar.

❖

if others also had to play after him.

The sailing ship navigated without ever sinking; its deck long and smooth like a glider.

When the moon winked, the captain of the ship told him that he should return home; for his parents would certainly worry if they did not find him.

Alejo said good-bye with great affection and, very strangely, without sadness; for he knew that he would be able to find them repeatedly in different parts of the world.

The trees, the river, the birds and his toys would be for him objects of eternal happiness.

He looked at the sea and wished to be home. He ran overjoyed to tell his sister about the marvelous trip that he had taken.

"Now we will never be bored" he said, "I discovered the far-off world and I've come to realize that what we wish for is right at hand; one has to know how to see and live, united with the beautiful things of the world."

And the children happily set out to play.

❖

Clemente Palma
Perú (1872 -1944)

The reader will certainly find the
following story different and unusual,
and it will not be long into the story
before the influence of Edgar Allan
Poe becomes apparent. Like the
American writer, Ricardo Palma's
story centers around a main obsession; in this case the eyes of his bride-
to-be, Lina, which serve as the focal
point throughout the entire story. The
author maintains interest by imparting
them a life of their own. Lina is depic-
ted as a beautiful and innocent young
girl, yet her eyes are devilish and tor-
turing, a paradox which keeps the
reader intrigued and in suspense until
the very last line of the story.

LOS OJOS DE LINA
Por Clemente Palma

El teniente Jym, de la armada inglesa, era nuestro amigo. Cuando entró en la Compañía Inglesa de Vapores le veíamos cada mes y pasábamos una o dos noches con él en alegre francachela. Jym había pasado gran parte de su juventud en Noruega, y era un insigne bebedor de whisky y de ajenjo; bajo la acción de estos licores le daba por cantar con voz estentórea lindas baladas escandinavas, que después nos traducía. Una tarde fuimos a despedirnos de él a su camarote, pues al día siguiente zarpaba el vapor para San Francisco. Jym no podía cantar en su cama a voz en cuello, como tenía costumbre, por razones de disciplina naval, y resolvimos pasar la velada refiriéndonos historias y aventuras de nuestra vida, sazonando las relaciones con repetidos sorbos de licor. Serían las dos de la mañana cuando terminamos los visitantes de Jym, nuestras relaciones; sólo Jym faltaba y le exigimos que hiciera la suya. Jym se arrellanó en un sofá; puso en una mesita próxima una pequeña botella de ajenjo y un aparato para destilar agua; encendió un puro y comenzó a hablar del modo siguiente:

No voy a referirles una balada ni una leyenda del Norte, como en otras ocasiones; hoy se trata de una historia verídica, de un episodio de mi vida de novio. Ya saben que, hasta hace dos años, he vivido en Noruega; por mi madre soy noruego, pero mi padre me hizo súbdito inglés. En Noruega me casé. Mi esposa se llama Axelina o Lina, como yo la llamo, y cuando tengan la ventolera de dar un paseo por Cristianía, vayan a mi casa, que mi esposa les

36

LINA'S EYES
By Clemente Palma

Lieutenant Jym of the English Navy was a friend of ours. When he first came and joined the English Steamship Company, we would see him every month and spend a night or two with him in a happy spree. Jym spent a great part of his youth in Norway, and he was a renowned consumer of whiskey and absinthe; and under the influence of these alcoholic beverages he would get the urge to sing with a stentorian voice beautiful Scandinavian ballads, which he would later translate for us. One afternoon we went to say good-bye to him in his cabin, since the following day his ship was weighing anchor and steaming out of port for San Francisco. Jym could not sing in his bed at the top of his lungs, as he was used to, for reasons of naval discipline, and we resolved to spend the night recounting amongst ourselves stories and adventures of our lives, spicing up the accounts with repeated sips of liquor. It must have been two in the morning when we, Jym's visitors, finished our narrations; it was Jym's turn and we urged him to tell his own. Jym made himself comfortable on the sofa; on a small table close-by he placed a small bottle of absinthe and an apparatus to distill water; lit a cigar and began to speak in the following manner:

"I'm not going to recount to you a ballad nor a legend from the Northern countries, like on other occasions; today it concerns a true story, from an episode of my life when I was dating. You all know that, up until two years ago, I have lived in Norway; on my mother's side I'm Norwegian, but my father made me an English subject. In Norway, I got married. My wife's name is Axelina, or Lina as I call her, and if you ever get a notion to take a trip around Cristiania, be sure to go to my home, where my wife will receive you with a great

37

hará con mucho gusto los honores.

Empezaré por decirles que Lina tenía los ojos más extrañamente endiablados del mundo. Ella tenía dieciséis años y yo estaba loco de amor por ella, pero profesaba a sus ojos el odio más rabioso que puede haber en corazón de hombre. Cuando Lina fijaba sus ojos en los míos me desesperaba, me sentía inquieto y con los nervios crispados; me parecía que alguien me vaciaba una caja de alfileres en el cerebro y que se esparcían a lo largo de mi espina dorsal; un frío doloroso galopaba por mis arterias, y la epidermis se me erizaba, como sucede a la generalidad de las personas al salir de un baño helado, y a muchas al tocar una fruta peluda, o al ver el filo de una navaja, o al rozar con las uñas el terciopelo, o al escuchar el *frufrú* de la seda o al mirar una gran profundidad. Esa misma sensación experimentaba al mirar los ojos de Lina. He consultado a varios médicos de mi confianza sobre este fenómeno y ninguno me ha dado la explicación; se limitaban a sonreír y a decirme que no me preocupara del asunto, que yo era un histérico, y no sé que otras majaderías. Y lo peor es que yo adoraba a Lina con exasperación, con locura, a pesar del efecto desastroso que me producían sus ojos. Y no se limitaban estos efectos a la tensión álgida de mi sistema nervioso; había algo más maravilloso aún, y es que cuando Lina tenía alguna preocupación o pasaba por ciertos estados psíquicos o fisiológicos, veía yo pasar por sus pupilas, al mirarme, en la forma vaga de pequeñas sombras fugitivas coronadas por puntitos de luz las ideas; sí, señores, las ideas. Estas entidades inmateriales e invisibles que tenemos todos o casi todos, pues hay muchos que no tienen ideas en la cabeza, pasaban por las pupilas de Lina con formas inexpresables. He dicho sombras porque es la palabra que más se acerca. Salían por detrás de la esclerótica, cruzaban la pupila y al llegar a la retina destellaban, y entonces sentía que en el fondo de mi cerebro respondía una dolorosa vibración de las células, surgiendo a su vez una idea dentro de mí.

Se me ocurría comparar los ojos de Lina al cristal de la claraboya de mi camarote, por el que veía pasar, al anochecer, a los peces azorados con la luz de mi lámpara, chocando sus estrafalarias cabezas contra el macizo cristal, que, por su espesor y convexidad,

deal of graciousness.

"I will begin by telling you that Lina had the most strangely dia-
bolical-looking eyes in the world. She was sixteen years old and I
was madly in love with her, but I felt toward her eyes the greatest
degree of hatred that could ever possibly fill the heart of a man.
When Lina would stare into my eyes I felt despair, uneasiness and
with my nerves on edge; I felt as though someone was emptying a
box of pins atop my brain and that these were spreading out the
length of my spinal cord; a painful sense of cold travelled at terrific
speed through my arteries, and my skin bristled, as so commonly
happens to most people when they come out of a cold bath, and to
many others upon touching a fuzzy fruit, or looking at the sharpness
of a blade, or touching velvet with their fingernails, or when hearing
the rustling noise of satin or looking down from a great height. That
very same sensation I would experience when I gazed into Lina's
eyes. I've consulted a number of what I consider to be trustworthy
doctors regarding this phenomena and none has given me an expla-
nation; they merely smile and tell me that I should not be concerned
about this matter; that I was hysterical, and I don't know what other
manner of nonsense. Yet the worse part is that I adored Lina with
exasperation, with madness, despite the disastrous effect that her
eyes had on me. And these effects were not limited to the algid state
of my nervous system; there was something even more amazing,
which was that when Lina experienced some preoccupation or when
she went through various psychic or physiological states, I would
see pass through her pupils, as she looked at me, in blurred forms,
like small fleeting shadows crowned by tiny points of light, ideas;
yes, my friends, ideas. These immaterial and invisible entities which
we all have –or most of us have, since many do not have ideas in
their head– would pass across Lina's pupils in inexpressible forms.
I said shadows because it is the most fitting word. They would come
out of the back of the sclera, then cross the pupil and upon arriving
at the retina they would flash, and then I felt that in the deepest part
of my brain a painful vibration of cells responded, which in turn
spurted forth an idea within me.

"It occurred to me to compare Lina's eyes with the glass pane of
the skylight in my cabin, through which, at nightfall, I could see fish
pass by, seemingly flustered by the light of my lamp, hitting their
bizarre looking heads against the heavy pane, which, due to its thick-

hacía borrosas y deformes sus siluetas. Cada vez que veía esa parranda de ideas en los ojos de Lina, me decía yo: "¡Vaya! ¡Ya están pasando los peces!" Sólo que éstos atravesaban de una modo misterioso la pupilas de mi amada y formaban su madriguera en las cavernas oscuras de mi encéfalo.

Pero bah!, soy un desordenado. Les hablo del fenómeno sin haberles descrito los ojos y las bellezas de mi Lina. Lina es morena y pálida; sus cabellos ondosos se rizaban en la nuca con tan adorable gracia, que jamás belleza de mujer alguna me sedujo tanto como el dorso del cuello de Lina, al sumergirse en la sedosa negrura de sus cabellos. Los labios, casi siempre entreabiertos, por cierta tirantez infantil del labio superior, eran tan rojos que parecían acostumbrados a comer fresas, a beber sangre o a depositar la de los intensos rubores; probablemente esto último, pues, cuando las mejillas se le encendían, palidecían aquellos. Bajos estos labios había unos dientes diminutos tan blancos, que le iluminaban la faz cuando un rayo de luz jugaba sobre ellos. Era para mí una delicia verla morder cerezas; de buena gana me hubiera dejado morder por aquella deliciosa boquita, a no ser por los ojos endemoniados que habitaban más arriba. ¡Esos ojos! Lina, repito, es morena, de cabello, cejas y pestañas negras. Si la hubieran visto dormida alguna vez, yo les hubiera preguntado: ¿De qué color creen que tiene Lina los ojos? A buen seguro que, guiados por el color de su cabellera, de sus cejas y pestañas me habrían respondido: negros. Qué chasco! Pues no, señor; los ojos tenían color, es claro, pero ni todos los oculistas del mundo, ni todos los pintores habrían acertado a determinarlo ni a reproducirlo. Eran de un corte perfecto, rasgados y grandes; debajo de ellos una línea azulada formaba la ojera y parecía como la tenue sombra de sus largas pestañas. Hasta aquí, como ven, nada hay de raro; éstos eran los ojos de Lina cerrados o entornados; pero una vez abiertos y lucientes las pupilas, allí de mis angustias. Nadie me quitará de la cabeza que Mefistófeles tenía su gabinete de trabajo detrás de esas pupilas. Eran ellas de un color que fluctuaba entre todos los de la gama, y sus más complicadas combinaciones. A veces me parecían dos grandes esmeraldas, alumbradas por detrás por luminosos carbunclos. Las figuraciones

ness and convex shape, rendered their silhouettes blurred and deformed. Every time I saw that crowd of ideas in Lina's eyes, I would say to myself: Look!, here come the fish again! Except that these would cross along the pupil of my beloved in a mysterious way, forming their burrow in the darkened caverns of my encephalon.

"But, let's face it! I am completely disorganized. For I speak to you of this phenomena without having first described to you the eyes and the overall beauty of Lina. Lina is dark-skinned, although also somewhat pale: her wavy hair curled at the base of her neck with such adorable grace, that never before had the beauty of a woman seduced me so much as the back of Lina's neck, as it submerged in the satin negritude of her hair. Her lips, almost always opened, because of a certain childlike twitch of the upper lip, were so red that they appear to be accustomed to eating strawberries, or drinking blood or being the site of all that could possibly have produced the most intense sensation of blushing; and indeed, it must have been the latter, since, when her cheeks turned bright red, everything else paled. Underneath those lips there were diminutive-sized teeth so white, they illuminated her face whenever a ray of light played on them. It was a delightful experience for me to see her bite into cherries; I would gladly have permitted myself to be bitten by that tiny and delicious-looking mouth, had it not been for those demon-possessed eyes located atop. Those eyes! Lina, I repeat, is dark-skinned, her hair, eyebrows and eyelashes black. If you should ever have seen her sleeping, I would have asked you: What do you think is the color of Lina's eyes? Certainly, given the color of her hair, her brows and eyelashes, you would have answered: black. How deceiving! Well, not at all; the eyes, of course, had color, but neither all the oculists, nor all the painters in the world could have correctly ascertained their true color, nor would they have been able to reproduce it. They were of a perfect shape, almond-eyed and large; the circles underneath each eye were of a bluish shaded pigment and appeared to be the subdued shadow of her eyebrows. So far, as you can see, there is nothing unusual; these were Lina's eyes either closed or half-closed; but once they were open and the pupils bright and shiny, that's when my anguish would begin. No one will get it out of my head that Mephistopheles had his workshop behind those pupils. They were of a color that fluctuated between all those in the spectrum in its most complex combinations. At times, they seemed to me two large emeralds, lit up from behind by luminous carbuncles. The greenish

verdosas y rojizas que despedían se erizaban poco a poco y pasaban por mil cambiantes, como las burbujas de jabón; luego venía
un color indefinible, pero uniforme, a cubrirlos todos, y en medio
palpitaba un puntito de luz, de lo más mortificante por los tonos
felinos y diabólicos que tomaba. Los hervores de la sangre de Lina,
sus tensiones nerviosas, sus irritaciones, sus placeres, los alambica-
mientos y juegos de su espíritu, se denunciaban por el color que
adquiría ese punto de luz misteriosa.

Con la continuidad de tratar a Lina llegué a traducir algo los
resplandores múltiples de sus ojos. Sus sentimentalismos de muchacha romántica eran verdes; sus alegrías, violáceas; sus celos,
amarillos, y rojos sus ardores de mujer apasionada. El efecto de
estos ojos en mí era desastroso. Tenían sobre mí un imperio horrible, y en verdad yo sentía mi dignidad de varón humillada con esta
especie de esclavitud misteriosa, ejercida sobre mi alma por esos
ojos que odiaba como a personas. En vano es que tratara de resis-
tir; los ojos de Lina me subyugaban, y sentía que me arrancaban el
alma para triturarla y carbonizarla entre dos chispazos de esta mirada de Luzbel. Por último, con el alma ardiente de amor y de ira,
tenía yo que bajar la mirada, porque sentía que mi mecanismo nervioso llegaba a torsiones desgarradoras, y que mi cerebro saltaba
de mi cabeza, como un abejorro encerrado dentro de un horno.
Lina no se daba cuenta del efecto desastroso que me hacían sus
ojos. Todo Cristianía se los elogiaba por hermosos y a nadie causa-
ban la impresión terrible que a mí; sólo yo estaba constituido para
ser la víctima de ellos. Yo tenía reacciones de orgullo; a veces
pensaba que Lina abusaba del poder que tenía sobre mí, y que se
complacía en humillarme; entonces mi dignidad de varón se suble-
vaba vengativa reclamando imaginarios fueros, y a mi vez me en-
tretenía en tiranizar a mi novia, exigiéndola sacrificios y mortifi-
cándola hasta hacerla llorar. En el fondo había una intención que
yo trataba de realizar disimuladamente; sí, en esta valiente suble-
vación contra la tiranía de esas pupilas estaba embozada mi cobardía; haciendo llorar a Lina la hacía cerrar los ojos, y cerrados los
ojos me sentía libre de mi cadena. Pero la pobrecilla ignoraba el
arma terrible que tenía contra mí; sencilla y canderosa, la buena
muchacha tenía un corazón de oro y me adoraba y me obedecía. Lo

and reddish flashes they emitted would turn little by little into an iris effect and would go through a thousand combinations, like soap bubbles; then an undefinable color would appear, but uniformly, to cover these completely, and in the middle palpitated a tiny point of light, of the most mortifying nature due to the feline and diabolical tone that it would take. Lina's seething blood, her nervous tension, her irritations, her pleasures, the excessive subtleties and fancies of her spirit, were exposed by the color which this mysterious point of light acquired.

"As time passed and as I got to know Lina better, I began to understand something about the brightness of her eyes. Her sentimentality, which was that of a young woman, was green; her joyfulness, of a violaceous color; her jealousies, yellow, and shades of red her ardor as a woman of passion. The effect of these eyes on me was disastrous. They had over me a horrible power, and in fact I felt my dignity as a man humiliated with that type of mysterious slavery, exercised over my soul by those eyes that I hated as if they were real people. It was useless for me to try to resist; Lina's eyes subjugated me, and I felt that they were tearing my soul apart in order to grind it to a pulp and burn it up between two sparks of Luzbel's glances. Finally, with my soul burning with love and ire, I had to lower my glance, because I felt as though my nervous system was reaching a state of unbearable contortions, and that my brain was jumping up and down inside my head, like a bumblebee trapped in an oven. Lina was not aware of the disastrous effect that her eyes had on me. The whole of Cristianía praised them for their beauty and they never seemed to have caused on anyone else such a negative or terrible impression as the one I have experienced. I alone, was the only victim of those eyes. I had reactions of pride; at times I thought that Lina abused the power she had over me, and that she derived pleasure from humiliating me; it was then that my male dignity would vengefully rebel, claiming imaginary privileges, and in my own way I amused myself by tyrannizing my loved one, demanding sacrifices from her and mortifying her till she cried. To be truthful, I had an ulterior motive which I was trying to bring about furtively; yes, in the valiant revolt against the tyranny of those pupils was my cowardice concealed: if I made Lina cry I would also get her to close her eyes, and when those eyes were closed I felt freed from my chain. But the poor little thing was unaware of the terrible weapon she had against me; simple and innocent, the good girl had a heart of gold

más curioso es que yo, que odiaba sus hermosos ojos, la quería por ellos. Aun cuando siempre salía vencido, volvía siempre a luchar contra esas terribles pupilas, con la esperanza de vencer. Cuántas veces las rojas fulguraciones del amor me hicieron el efecto de cien cañonazos disparados contra mis nervios! Por amor propio no quise revelar a Lina mi esclavitud.

Nuestros amores debían tener una solución como la tienen todos: o me casaba con Lina o rompía con ella. Esto último era imposible, luego tenía que casarme con Lina. Lo que me aterraba de la vida de casado, era la perduración de esos ojos que tenían que alumbrar terriblemente mi vejez. Cuando se acercaba la época en que debía pedir la mano de Lina a su padre, un rico armador, la obsesión de los ojos de ella me era insoportable. De noche los veía fulgurar como ascuas en la oscuridad de mi alcoba; veía el techo y allí estaban terribles y porfiados; miraba la pared y estaban incrustados allí; cerraba los ojos y los veía adheridos sobre mis párpados con una tenacidad luminosa tal, que su fulgor iluminaba el tejido de arterias y venillas de la membrana. Al fin, rendido, dormía, y las miradas de Lina llenaban mi sueño de redes que se apretaban y me estrangulaban el alma. ¿Qué hacer? Formé mis planes; pero no sé si por orgullo, amor, o por una noción del deber muy grabada en mi espíritu, jamás pensé en renunciar a Lina.

El día en que la pedí, Lina estaba contentísima. ¡Oh, cómo brillaban sus ojos y qué endiabladamente! La estreché en mis brazos delirante de amor, y al besar sus labios sangrientos y tibios tuve que cerrar los ojos casi desvanecido.

—¡Cierra los ojos, Lina mía, te lo ruego!

Lina sorprendida, los abrió más, y al verme pálido y descompuesto me preguntó asustada, cogiéndome las manos:

—¿Qué tienes, Jym?... Habla. ¡Dios Santo!... ¿Estás enfermo? Habla.

—No..., perdóname; nada tengo, nada... le respondí sin mirarla.

—Mientes, algo te pasa...

—Fue un vagido, Lina..., ya pasará...

—¿Y por qué querías que cerrara los ojos? ¿No quieres que te

and she adored and obeyed me. The most curious thing about all of this is that I, who hated her beautiful eyes, loved her because of them. Even though I always turned out the loser, again and again I would try to fight those terrible pupils, with the hope of conquering them. There were several times when those reddish flashes of love had upon me the effect of a hundred cannon shots fired at my nervous system. Because of self respect I did not want to reveal my enslavement to Lina.

"The love that we shared had to have a solution as all love does: That is, either I got married to Lina or I broke off with her. The latter was impossible, so I just had to get married to Lina. That which terrorized me about married life, however, was the long length of time that those eyes were to illuminate in such a terrible way my old age. When the proper time neared in which I should ask Lina's father, a wealthy shipowner, for her hand in marriage, the obsession that I had with her eyes became intolerable. At night I would see them glow like live coal in the darkness of my bedroom; I would look up at the ceiling and there they were terrifying and persistent; I would look toward the wall and they were encrusted there; I would close my eyes and I would see them adhered to my eyelids with such luminous tenacity, that their glow lit up the web of arteries and small veins within its membrane. Finally, exhausted, I would fall asleep, and Lina's glances would fill my dream with nets that tightened up and strangled my soul. What could I do? I made my plans; but I don't know if because of pride, love, or a sense of duty deeply ingrained in my spirit, I never once thought of abandoning Lina.

"The day I asked for her hand, Lina was extremely happy. Oh, how her eyes shined and with such bedevilment! I embraced her delirious with love and upon kissing her warm and blood-red lips I had to close my eyes almost in a faint.

"Close your eyes, Lina dear, I implore you.

"Lina somewhat surprised, opened them even wider, and upon seeing me pale and upset asked me fearfully, grabbing me by the hands:

'What's the matter, Jym!... Say something. Holy God! Are you sick? Say something'.

"No..., forgive me; there's nothing wrong with me, nothing... I answered without looking at her."

'You're lying, something is wrong with you'.

"It was a dizzy spell, Lina..., it will go away."

'And why did you want me to close my eyes? Don't you want me to look at you, dear one?'

mire, bien mío?

No respondí y la miré medroso. ¡Oh¡, allí estaban esos ojos terribles, con todos sus insoportables chiporroteos de sorpresa, de amor y de inquietud. Lina, al notar mi turbado silencio, se alarmó más. Se sentó sobre mis rodillas, cogió mi cabeza entre sus manos y dijo con violencia:

—No, Jym, tú me engañas, algo extraño pasa en ti desde hace algún tiempo: tú has hecho algo malo, pues sólo los que tienen un peso en la conciencia no se atreven a mirar de frente. Yo te conoceré en los ojos, mírame, mírame.

Cerré los ojos y la besé en la frente.

—No me beses; mírame, mírame.

—!Oh, por Dios, Lina, déjame!...

—¿Y por qué no me miras? —insistió casi llorando.

Yo sentía honda pena de mortificarle y a la vez mucha vergüenza de confesarle mi necedad: «No te miro, porque tus ojos me asesinan; porque les tengo un miedo cerval, que no me explico, ni puedo reprimir.» Callé, pues, y me fui a mi casa, después que Lina dejo la habitación llorando.

Al día siguiente, cuando volví a verla, me hicieron pasar a su alcoba: Lina había amanecido enferma con angina. Mi novia estaba en cama y la habitación casi oscura. ¡Cuánto me alegré de esto último! Me senté junto al lecho y le hablé apasionadamente de mis proyectos para el futuro. En la noche había pensado que lo mejor para que fuéramos felices era confesarle mis ridículos sufrimientos. Quizá podríamos ponernos de acuerdo... Usando anteojos negros... quizá. Después que le referí mis dolores, Lina se quedó un momento en silencio.

—¡Bah, qué tontería! fue todo lo que contestó.

Durante veinte días no salió Lina de la cama y había orden del médico que no me dejaran entrar. El día en que Lina se levantó me mandó llamar. Faltaban pocos días para nuestra boda, y ya había recibido infinidad de regalos de sus amigos y parientes. Me llamó Lina para mostrarme el vestido de azahares, que le habían traído durante su enfermedad, así como los obsequios. La habitación estaba envuelta en una oscura penumbra en la que apenas podía yo ver a Lina; se sentó en un sofá de espaldas a la entornada ventana,

"I did not answer her and looked at her with apprehension. Oh, there they were, those terrible eyes, with all their unbearable sparks of surprise, love and uneasiness. Lina, upon noticing my uncomfortable silence, became even more alarmed. She sat on my knees, grasped my head in her hands and said to me angrily:

'No, Jym, you are deceiving me, something strange has been happening to you for quite some time: you have done something wrong, since only those who have a great weight on their conscience do not dare to look at someone in the eye. I shall find out by looking into your eyes, look at me, look at me.'

"I closed my eyes and kissed her on the forehead."

'Don't kiss me; look at me, look at me.'

"Oh, for God sake, Lina, leave me alone!"

'And why don't you look at me?' she insisted almost crying.

"I deeply wished not to mortify her and at the same time felt a great deal of shame in confessing my foolishness. 'I don't look at you, because your eyes kill me; because I'm scared to death, which I can't explain nor repress.' So I said no more, and went home, after Lina had left the room crying.

"The following day, when I saw her again, they let me in her bedroom: Lina had awakened ill with angina. My bride-to-be was in bed and the room was semi-dark. How happy I was in regard to the latter! I sat next to the bed and spoke to her passionately about my future projects. During the night I had thought it would be best for our own happiness if I were to confess to her my ridiculous anguish. Perhaps we could reach some understanding... Using dark glasses... perhaps. After I related my pain to her, Lina remained silent for a while."

'Pooh, what nonsense!' was all she said.

"During twenty days Lina did not get out of bed and by doctor's orders I was not allowed to enter. The day that Lina got up she sent for me. Only a few days remained before our wedding, and she had already received countless gifts from her friends and relatives. Lina asked me to stop by so she could show me the dress with tiny orange blossoms, that she had received during her illness, as well as the presents. The room was shrouded in semidarkness, so that I barely could see Lina; she had seated herself in a high-back sofa next to the half-closed window and began to show me necklaces, dresses, some alabaster doves, trinkets, earrings, and I don't know how many

y comenzó a mostrarme brazaletes, sortijas, collares, vestidos, unas palomas de alabastro, dijes, zarcillos y no sé qué cuánta preciosidad. Allí estaba el regalo de su padre, el viejo armador: consistía en un pequeño yate de paseo, es decir, no estaba el yate, sino el documento de propiedad: mis regalos también estaban y también el que Lina me hacía, consistente en una cajita de cristal de roca, forrada con terciopelo rojo.

Lina me alcanzaba sonriente los regalos, y yo, con galantería de enamorado, le besaba la mano. Por fin, trémula, me alcanzó la cajita:

—Mírala a la luz —me dijo—, son piedras preciosas, cuyo brillo conviene apreciar debidamente.

Y tiró de una hoja de la ventana. Abrí la caja y se me erizaron los cabellos de espanto: debí ponerme monstruosamente pálido. Levanté la cabeza horrorizado y vi a Lina que me miraba fijamente con unos ojos negros, vidriosos e inmóviles. Una sonrisa, entre amorosa e irónica, plegaba los labios de mi novia, hechos con zumos de fresas silvestres. Salté desesperado y cogí violentamente a Lina de la mano.

—¿Qué has hecho, desdichada?

—¡Es mi regalo de boda!» respondió tranquilamente.

Lina estaba ciega. Como huéspedes azorados estaban en los cuencas unos ojos de cristal, y los suyos, los de mi Lina, esos ojos extraños que me habían mortificado tanto, me miraban amenazadores y burlones desde el fondo de la caja roja, con la misma mirada endiablada de siempre...

Cuando terminó Jym, quedamos todos en silencio, profundamente conmovidos. En verdad que la historia era terrible. Jym tomó un vaso de ajenjo y se lo bebió de un trago. Luego nos miró con aire melancólico. Mis amigos miraban, pensativos, el uno la claraboya del camarote y el otro la lámpara que se bamboleaba a los balances del buque. De pronto, Jym soltó una carcajada burlona, que cayó como un enorme cascabel en medio de nuestras meditaciones.

—¡Hombres de Dios! ¿Creen ustedes que haya mujer alguna capaz del sacrificio que les he referido? Si los ojos de una mujer les hacen daño, ¡Saben cómo lo remediará ella? Pues arrancándoles

other things of great value. There too was the gift her father, the elderly shipowner, had given her: it consisted of a small pleasure yacht, that is, the yacht wasn't there, rather the deed of ownership; my gifts were there too and also the one Lina was giving me, which consisted of a small box made of rock crystal, lined inside with red velvet.

"Lina, all the while smiling, would hand me the gifts, and I, with all the gallantry of a person in love, would kiss her hand. At last, trembling, she handed me the little box:

'Look at it in the light' she said to me, 'These are precious stones, whose brightness should be fully appreciated.'

"And she opened the other half of the window. I opened the box and my hair stood on end from the fright that I experienced: I must have turned extremely pale. Horrified, I raised my head and saw Lina staring at me with black colored eyes, glassy and still. A smile, half amorous, half ironic, revealed itself on the lips of my intended, made from the juice of wild strawberries. I jumped up in despair and grabbed Lina violently by the hand:

"What have you done, your poor thing?"

'It is my wedding gift!' she replied quite calmly.

"Lina was blind. In the eye sockets, a pair of glass eyes moved about like some confused guests and her real eyes, those of my beloved Lina, those strange eyes that had mortified me so much, were looking at me menacingly and mockingly from the bottom of the red box with the same diabolical look of always."

When Jym finished, we all remained silent, profoundly moved. This was truly a terrible story. Jym took a glass of absinthe and drank it in one gulp. Then he looked at us wistfully. My friends were looking around, pensively, one at the cabin's skylight and the other at the lamp that swayed with the ship's rocking motion. Suddenly, Jym let out a loud, mocking laugh that fell on all present like an enormous rattlesnake in the middle of our meditations.

"Good God,! Do you really believe that there could exist a woman capable of the type of sacrifice that I have just related to you? If the eyes of a woman were harmful, do you know how she would remedy this? Well, by tearing out *yours* so that you would not be able to see hers. No; dear friends, I have told you an improb-

los suyos para que no vean los de ella. No; amigos míos, les he referido una historia inverosímil cuyo autor tengo el honor de presentarles.

Y nos mostró, levantándola en alto, su botellita de ajenjo, que parecía una solución concentrada de esmeraldas.

❖

able story whose author I am now pleased to present to you."

And he showed us, raising it on high, his small bottle of absinthe, which appeared to be a concentrated solution of emeralds.

❖

Francisco Barnoya Gálvez
(Guatemala)

The following story vividly reflects the psychology, customs and traditions of rural Latin America: veneration for the elders, pride and love of homeland, a deep sense of community, propensity to hard work, the exhilarating sense of freedom born of the boundless horizons of open country; as well as a deeply ingrained belief in the supernatural and a tendency to dramatically justify all eventful happenings taking place in the daily lives of its inhabitants.

The dramatic incidents represented in this story are graphically represented by the black butterfly which opens and closes the story in a perfect circle, imparting a tone of impending doom to the entire narration.

LA MARIPOSA NEGRA

Por Francisco Barnoya Gálvez

Daba a Juan Mayén -caporal de la finca "El Caimito"-, y quien, según el decir de las gentes del lugar, era el vaquero más "tres piedras" de todos los contornos, las últimas órdenes relativas a las faenas del día, cuando una mariposa negra, grande, de una dimensión aproximada a los veinte centímetros, pasó volando tan cerca de mí que rozó el ala gacha de mi sombrero tejano. Como un avión que por fin llega al término del viaje, la mariposa negra se introdujo a su hangar improvisado que vino a ser el cuarto de mi abuelo, situado, precisamente, a espaldas mías en la situación en que me hallaba colocado.

No di importancia alguna a incidente tan vulgar en los trópicos, y seguí dando mis órdenes:

–Tú, Juan Mayén, te vas con tu gente a la quebrada del Tigrillo y me la pones a trabajar macizo. Ya sabes que me gusta que los trabajos me los hagan bien y aprisa...

Pero mis palabras no pudieron seguir pronunciándose. Juan Mayén, a quien dirigí la vista al pronunciar la última, tiritaba entero, como si fuera presa de los intensos calofríos que preceden siempre a la llegada de las calenturas. Su rostro de criollo fornido y bien hecho se había colorado con una palidez semejante a la de la cera sin refinar.

–¿Qué te pasa a tí, Juan Mayén? –le dije– . ¿A tí, Juan Mayén, que no tiemblas ni cuando montas por primera vez a las potrancas cerreras, que ahora tiemblas con sólo haber visto una mariposa negra? ¡Te estás poniendo viejo, Juan Mayén! Si sigues así, cuidate, porque te la va a ganar el Pedro Cansinos... Y vaya que le lleva ganas a ganártela...

THE BLACK BUTTERFLY

By Francisco Barnoya Gálvez

I was giving Juan Mayen, foreman of the «El Caimito» farm, who, according to people of the area, was the most able cowboy of the area, the latest orders relative to the duties of the day, when a large, black butterfly, of approximately twenty centimeters in size, flew past me at such close proximity that it almost grazed the turned-down brim of my Texan hat. Like an airplane arriving at its final destination, the black butterfly landed into its makeshift hangar which happened to be my grandfather's room, located directly opposite where I was standing at the moment.

I did not attach much importance to this incident, being so common in the tropics, and continued to give my orders:

"You, Juan Mayen, go with your crew to the Tigrillo gorge and really put them to work. You know that I like that work assignments be done well and promptly..."

But I was unable to continue saying those words. As I was uttering the last word, I looked at Juan Mayen and saw that he was shivering all over, as if seized with the intense shivers that always precede the outbreak of fever. His face, that of a robust and strong creole, turned into a color resembling the paleness of unrefined wax.

"What is the matter with you, Juan Mayen?" I said to him. "You, the Juan Mayen who never trembles even when mounting untamed young fillies for the first time, but now trembles at the mere sight of a black butterfly. You're getting old, Juan Mayen! You'd better be on your guard, because, if you keep this up, Pedro Cansinos will outdo you... And let me tell you, he's really determined to outdo you..."

–Si no es miedo, patrón, lo que tengo. Es una simple corazonada y por eso tiemblo: aquí va a haber difunto, patroncito. La misma mariposa así de grande –con sus manos renegrecidas me diseñaba las dimensiones–, negra como la boca del coyote, pasó por aquí cuando para las lluvias de octubre se murió la difunta niña Raimunda, la segunda mujer del patrón grande, de su abuelo mi señor don Chema... La misma llegó al rancho de la Tomasa hace ocho días, y ya ve que esa misma tarde la venadearon al Efraín en la quebrada de los tempisques... No son cuentos ni chiles, patrón, es la pura verdad; cuando llega la mariposa negra, seguro que hay difunto... No voy a saberlo yo que hace treinta años que vivo en la costa amansando potrancas y potros cimarrones...

–No seas papo, Juan Mayén. Esas son puras sonseras. A ustedes siempre se los engatuzan las viejas con sus chiles. Andáte luego a trabajar y no pienses más en mariposas, ni pendejadas. Ve que yo quiero que me dejen hoy limpio el potrero...

Di media vuelta, lo dejé con el estribillo en la boca de que aquí va a haber difunto; solté una estentórea carcajada; y grité: –Tú, Lupe –tal es el diminutivo de mi mozo–, ensíllame a la Sapuyula con la montura mexicana; ponéme bastimiento en las alforjas; y prepárate tú también para salir, porque vamos a pasar todo el día en los potreros de Bran.

Tras breve momentos de espera, jinete ya en mi yegua Sapuyula, en cuyos ijares sudados hincaba con mis espuelas de plata de carrera, partimos, como alma que se lleva el diablo, con dirección a los potreros de lo de Bran, en donde me esperaban un día de incesante trabajo y la cuadrilla presta a acatar mis órdenes.

Dando órdenes, perdido entre los grandes zacatonales de los potreros de la finca pasé todo el día gritando:

–Aquí me van a arriar las vacas paridas. Para allá echen los toretes...; en este cerco hay que colocar las piedras que se han caido...; en el de allá, donde están las bateas con sal, echen a los novillos que se van a castrar pronto...

Allí, metido dentro de mi campo verde y criollo, respirando a pulmón lleno el aire caliente y enrarecido de las tierras bajas de mi trópico excelso, pasé todo el día. ¡Oh!, alegría sublime de sentirse dueño de inmensas –tan inmensas, que sus limites se pierden en el

"What I have isn't fear master. It's simply a feeling in my heart and that's why I tremble: there's going to be a death, master. The same butterfly, and it was this big" –indicating with his deeply darkened hands its dimensions–, "and black as the mouth of a coyote, passed through here during the October rains about the time when young mistress Raimunda, the second wife of the head master, that is of your grandfather Don Chema, died. The same one arrived at the Tomasa ranch some eight days ago and, as you know, that same afternoon they ambushed Efraín at the Tempisque Tree gorge. These are not tales nor lies, master, it's the honest truth; when the black butterfly comes, for sure there is death. If there's someone that should know about these things it's me after having lived some 30 years on the coast here taming fillies and wild colts."

"Don't be a fool, Juan Mayén. That's plain silliness. Old women always lead you astray with their lies. So get to work and stop thinking about butterflies and other nonsense. Get going, I want all of you to finish cleaning the colt stalls today."

I turned around and left him mumbling the same old refrain about "there going to be a death here in the family"; I let out a stentorian laugh, and shouted: "You, Lupe," –which is the diminutive of my servant's name– "saddle up Sapuyula with the Mexican saddle; put provisions for me in the saddlebags; and get ready to go also, because we are going to spend the whole day at Brand's stud farm."

After a few brief moments of waiting, mounted on my mare Sapuyula, into whose perspiring flanks I trusted my silver racing spurs, we rode off as if the devil were on our tail, in the direction of Bran's ranch where a full day's work and a crew of workers ready to obey my orders were awaiting me.

Lost among the tall pasture grass of the filly grazing areas, I spent the entire day shouting orders:

"Over here drive the cows that have recently calved ... Over there you can put the young bulls...; put back the rocks that have fallen off from this fence. In that one over there, where the salt troughs are, put the bullocks that are soon to be castrated..."

Out there, in the midst of my verdant creole countryside taking in deep full breaths of the hot and rarefied air of my sublime tropical land, I spent the entire day. Oh! supreme happiness of feeling lord and master of such vastly immense –so immense, that their limits disappear on the far off blue and green of the horizon– grasslands of

horizonte verde y azul– sabanas de ese llano verde mío, infinitamente verde, verde como las bandadas de loros que pasaban hablando un lenguaje sin sentido sobre mí, verde como las alas del quetzal, verdes como las hojas de mi milpa maya... De ese llano prolífico, como las mujeres, y como los animals, y como los hombres, y como todo lo de mi tierra guatemalteca... Dueño y señor de ese llano que fue haciendo suyo, palmo a palmo don José María Berduo Rajax –raro engendro de un castellano y de una india neta– hasta llegar a formar la vasta extensión de trescientas caballerías que ahora forman parte de la finca "El Caimito"...

Sentí ansias de gritar: todo esto es mío, el campo, los hombres, las montañas y las bestias, y, en un loco frenesí de estúpido dominio –pasión que se apodera del hombre en los trópicos ante la grandeza de su exuberación– hinqué espuelas a mi bestia y, como un centauro criollo, recorrí quién sabe cuántas leguas.

Rendido, fatigado, cubierto el rostro con esa pasta achocolatada que se forma de la conjunción del sudor con nuestra tierra trigüeña como una mengala, volvía, cumplidas ya todas mis labores, a la casa de la finca. La Sapuyula, feliz de retornar a la querencia, daba trancos largos, sin necesitar que yo la fustigara.

Caminaba, caminaba, añudando horizontes...

Entonando una canción criolla y haciendo caracolear mi yegua llegué triunfal, a los patios de mi finca. En mi llegada encontraba siempre –exquisita recepción– la algarabía peculiar de las casas de finca, el aroma delicado de las tortillas que sahuman el ambiente y los cantos de los vaqueros frente a la fogata en que calientan el café. Pero ahora todo estaba sumido en el más absoluto de los silencios. Ni siquiera el mastín de mis afectos vino a lamer el polvo de mis polainas.

Una inquietud grande se apoderó de mí. Bajé de la bestia y corrí. A trancos largos subí los escalones que conducen al corredor de la casa. Estaba ya en ellos, cuando la Juana, la vieja ama de llaves que nos vio nacer y nos cuidó en la infancia, con voz llorosa, y con la mueca del dolor, me dijo con palabras entrecortadas:

–¡Qué gran desgracia, patroncito! ¡Al patrón grande, a mi señor don Chema, su abuelito, lo han traído en unas angarillas, muerto! Los mismos niños de don Güicho López, los dueños del "Coyolar",

those green plains of mine, so infinitely green, green as the flocks of parrots flying overhead, speaking a meaningless language, green as the wings of the quetzal, green as the leaves of my Mayan cornfield... Of that fertile plain as prolific as its women, its animals and its men and like everything else in my Guatemalan homeland... Lord and master of that plain conquered inch by inch by the character and constancy of my grandfather Don Jose María Berduo Rajas –a rare offspring of a Spanish father and a pure Indian mother– and which was to eventually become the vast 300 acres area which now makes up "El Caimito" ranch.

I felt like shouting: all of this is mine, the fields, the men, the mountains and the beasts, and in one impetuous frenzy of senseless dominance –a passion that obsesses a man born in the tropics before the grandeur of its exuberance– I dug my spurs into my beast and, like a creole centaur, rode who knows how many miles.

Exhausted, fatigued, my face covered with that chocolate colored paste that comes from perspiration mixed with the earth of our native land, golden brown as an Indian girl, and having completed my tasks I was returning to the house on the ranch. Sapuyula, happy to return to her familiar stomping ground was taking long strides, without any need of my lashing or whipping her.

I kept going and going my eyes fixed on the horizon.

Intoning a creole song and making my mare prance I reached, exhilarated, the ranch grounds. Upon my arrival I was always met with –and what an exquisite reception– the hustle and bustle of everyday ranch life, the delicate aroma of tortillas perfuming the air and the songs of cowhands heating coffee next to a bonfire. But this time everything was surrounded by the most absolute silence.

Not even my beloved dog came to lick the dust of my gaiter.

A great uneasiness took hold of me. I got down from the animal and dashed up the stairs that lead to the hallway of the house. I was halfway up when Juana, our old housekeeper who had looked over us when we were children, with a tearful voice and a pained look on her face, said to me with faltering words:

"What a great misfortune, sir! They have brought the head master, my dear don Chema, your grandfather, on a stretcher, dead! It was Don Qüicho López' children themselves, owners of the "Coyolar" ranch, who found him lying on the ground on the road

lo encontraron tirado en el camino de Brito, y con sus mozos lo trajeron para acá. Dicen que a ellos se les figura que la bestia se le encabritó, tumbándolo en el suelo en el cual se debe haber descoyuntado. Tan bueno que era mi señor don Chema –Dios lo haya perdonado y lo tenga en su santa gloria–. Yo tanto que se lo decía que a sus años ya no debía salir solo; pero el se creía patojo, y hasta que se quedó con la suya de que le pasara algo...

Frío, completamente frío, por el susto que me produjo la noticia, llegué hasta el cuarto de mi abuelo. Allí, tendido en su catre de tijeras, que él no quiso abandonar nunca, estaba su cuerpo largo y macizo, de criollo bien hecho, y al cual la muerte, por una inconcebible ironía del destino, lo encontró de bruces.

Cuatro velas de cera y el plañidero gimotear de dos o tres rancheras eran su única companía...

Una sábana blanca, tan blanca como las nubes de mayo, cubría su cuerpo, y sobre ésta se posaba tranquila, como un emblema bordado exprofeso, la Mariposa Negra...

❖

from Brito, and with their servants brought him here. They believe that the animal must have reared up and knocked him down to the ground, and that must be the way he was injured. And don Chemas was such a good man —may God have mercy on his soul–. I kept telling him that at his age he should not go out alone anymore; but he always thought himself a young man, and he had his way, but look what happened?"

Feeling cold, utterly cold from the shock of the news, I reached my grandfather's room. There, stretched on the camp bed he refused to relinguish, was his long and stoutly built body, that of a creole, and whose neck never bent before anyone, and which by an inconceivable twist of fate death found lying flat on his face.

Four wax candles and the mournful sobbing of two or three ranch women were his only company...

A white sheet, as white as the clouds of May, covered his body, and on this sheet rested unperturbed, like an eloquent emblematic embroidery, the Black Butterfly...

❖

Horacio Quiroga
Uruguay (1878-1937)

In the previous story selected for
this anthology: *The Parrot who lost
its feathers,* the author relates a story
that is humorous, warm but inconse-
quential, that is to say in which there
is no didactic intent, and whose sole
objective appears to be the entertain-
ment of the reader. The following
story, however, has a more reflective
and serious tone. It is narrated in the
manner of a fable, in which love is
equated with responsibility, freedom
with work, personal interest with the
well-being of the community. It re-
mains warm and intense but in a more
dramatic way, introducing the child
to the real world in which he must
now become an active participant and
not merely a passive witness.

LA ABEJA HARAGANA
Por Horacio Quiroga

Había una vez en una colmena una abeja que no quería trabajar. Es decir, recorría los árboles uno por uno para tomar el jugo de las flores: pero en vez de conservarlo para convertirlo en miel, se lo tomaba todo.

Era pues, una abeja haragana. Todas las mañanas, apenas el sol calentaba el aire, la abejita se asomaba a la puerta de la colmena, veía que hacía buen tiempo, se peinaba con las patas, como hacen las moscas, y echaba entonces a volar, muy contenta del lindo día. Zumbaba muerta de gusto de flor en flor, entraba en la colmena, volvía a salir, y así se lo pasaba todo el día, mientras las otras abejas se mataban trabajando para llenar la colmena de miel, porque la miel es el alimento de las abejas recién nacidas.

Como las abejas son muy serias, comenzaron a disgustarse con el proceder de la hermana haragana. En la puerta de las colmenas hay siempre unas cuantas abejas que están de guardia para cuidar que no entren bichos en la colmena. Estas abejas suelen ser muy viejas, con gran experiencia de la vida, y tienen el lomo pelado porque han perdido todos los pelos de rozar contra la puerta de la colmena.

Un día, pues, detuvieron a la abeja haragana cuando iba a entrar, diciéndole:

—Compañera: es necesario que trabajes, porque todas la abejas debemos trabajar.

La abejita contestó

—Yo ando todo el día volando, y me canso mucho.

—No es cuestión de que te canses mucho —respondieron— sino

THE LAZY BEE

By Horacio Quiroga

Once upon a time there was a bee in a hive that didn't want to work. That is, it would go from tree to tree, drinking the nectar of the flowers; but instead of saving it and converting it into honey, she would drink it all up.

You could say she was a lazy bee. Every morning, just as the sun barely started to warm the air, the little bee would peek out of the door of the hive, and seeing that the weather was nice outside, she would comb herself with her legs, as flies do, and then fly off, pleased with the beautiful day. Bubbling with joy, she would buzz around from flower to flower, go in and out of the hive, and spend the entire day in this way, while the other bees would practically kill themselves striving to fill the hive with honey, because honey is the nourishment of all newly-born bees.

Since bees are so serious, they began to get upset with the behavior of their lazy sister bee. At the door of all beehives there are always a few bees guarding the entrance to prevent creepy-crawly bugs from entering the hive. These bees are usually quite old, and with great experience in life, and their back is bare because they've lost all their hair from constant rubbing against the doorway.

So one day, when the lazy bee was about to enter, they stopped her and said:

"Friend: you need to work, because all bees must work."

The little bee answered:

"I spend the whole day flying around, and I get very tired."

"It's not a question of your getting very tired" –they replied–

de que trabajes un poco. Es la primera advertencia que te hacemos.

Y diciendo eso la dejaron pasar.

Pero la abeja haragana no se corregía. De modo que a la tarde siguiente, las abejas que estaban de guardia le dijeron:

—Hay que trabajar, hermana.

Y ella respondió en seguida:

—¡Uno de estos días lo voy a hacer!

—No es cuestión de que lo hagas unos de estos días —le respondieron— sino mañana mismo. Acuérdate de esto.

Al anochecer siguiente se repitió la misma cosa. Antes de que le dijeran nada, la abejita declaró :

—¡Sí, sí, hermanitas! ¡Ya me acuerdo de lo que he prometido!

—No es cuestión de que te acuerdes de lo prometido —le respondieron— sino de que trabajes. Hoy es el 19 de abril. Pues bien: trata de que mañana, 20, hayas traído una gota siguiera de miel. Y ahora pasa.

Y diciendo eso se apartaron para dejarla entrar.

Pero el 20 de abril pasó en vano como todos los demás. Con la diferencia de que al caer el sol el tiempo se descompuso y comenzó a soplar el viento frío.

La abejita haragana voló apresurada hacia su colmena, pensando en lo calentito que estaría dentro. Pero cuando quiso entrar, las abejas que estaban de guardia se lo impidieron.

—No se entra —le dijeron fríamente.

—¡Yo quiero entrar! clamó la abejita—. Ésta es mi colmena.

—Ésta es la colmena de unas pobres abejas trabajadoras —le contestaron las otras—. No hay entrada para las haraganas.

—¡Mañana sin falta voy a trabajar! —insistió la abejita.

—No hay mañana para las que no trabajan —respondieron las abejas, que saben mucho de filosofía.

Y esto diciendo la empujaron fuera.

La abejita, sin saber qué hacer voló un rato aún; pero ya la noche caía, y se veía apenas. Quiso cogerse de una hoja, y cayó al suelo. Tenía el cuerpo entumecido por el aire frío, y no podía volar más.

Arrastrándose entonces por el suelo, trepando y bajando de los

"but that you do some work. It is our first warning to you."

And having said this they let her through.

But the lazy bee still would not mend her ways. So on the following afternoon, the bees that were on guard duty told her:

"One must work, sister bee."

And she replied right away:

"One of these days I'll do that."

"It's not a question of your doing it one of these days, but that you begin tomorrow. Keep this in mind."

And they let her through.

At nightfall the following day the same thing happened. Before anyone could say anything, the little bee exclaimed:

"Yes, yes, sister bees! I remember what I promised!"

"It's not a question of your remembering what you promised" they all answered "but that you do some work. Today is the 19th of April. Well then: see if on the 20th you can at least bring in one drop of honey. Now you can come in."

And having said this they stepped aside so she could enter.

But the 20th of April went by fruitlessly like all the others. With the difference that as the sun was going down the weather changed for the worse and a cold wind began to blow.

The lazy bee flew hurriedly towards the hive, thinking about how warm it would be there inside. But when she tried to enter, the bees which were on duty stopped her.

"You can't go in" they told her coldly.

"I want to go in!" cried out the little bee. "This is my hive".

"This is the hive of some poor hard-working bees" the others answered her. "We don't let in the lazy ones".

"Tomorrow without fail I am going to work!" insisted the little bee.

"There is no tomorrow for those that don't work" replied the other bees, who know a great deal about philosophy.

And having said this, they pushed her outside.

The little bee, not knowing what to do, flew a while still; but night was falling, and you could hardly see anything. She tried to hold on to a leaf, but fell to the ground. Her body was numb from the cold, and she could not fly anymore.

And so, dragging herself along the ground, climbing up and down

palitos y piedritas, que le parecían montañas, llegó a la puerta de la colmena, a tiempo que comenzaban a caer frías gotas de lluvia.

–¡Ay, mi Dios! –exclamó la desamparada–. Va a llover, y me voy a morir de frío!

Y tentó entrar en la colmena.

Pero de nuevo le cerraron el paso.

–¡Perdón! –gimió la abeja–. ¡Déjenme entrar!

–Ya es tarde –le respondieron.

–¡Por favor, hermanas! ¡Tengo sueño!

–Es más tarde aún.

–¡Compañeras, por piedad! ¡Tengo frío!

–Imposible.

–¡Por última vez! ¡Me voy a morir!

Entonces le dijeron:

–No, no morirás. Aprenderás en una sola noche lo que es el descanso ganado con el trabajo. Vete.

Y la echaron.

Entonces, temblando de frío, con las alas mojadas y tropezando, la abeja se arrastró hasta que de pronto rodó por un agujero; cayó rodando, mejor dicho, al fondo de una caverna.

Creyó que no iba a concluir nunca de bajar. Al fin llegó al fondo, y se halló bruscamente ante una víbora, una culebra verde de lomo color ladrillo, que la miraba enroscada y presta a lanzarse sobre ella.

En verdad, aquella caverna era el hueco de un árbol que habían transplantado hacía tiempo, y que la culebra había elegido por guarida.

Las culebras comen abejas, que les gustan mucho. Por esto la abejita, al encontrarse ante su enemiga, murmuró cerrando los ojos:

–¡Adiós mi vida! Ésta es la última hora que yo veo la luz.

Pero con gran sorpresa suya, la culebra no solamente no la devoró, sino que le dijo:

–¿Qué tal abejita? No has de ser muy trabajadora para estar aquí a estas horas.

–Es cierto –murmuró la abeja–. No trabajo, y yo tengo la culpa.

–Siendo así –agregó la culebra burlona –voy a quitar del mundo un mal bicho como tú. Te voy a comer abeja.

La abeja, temblando, exclamó entonces:

small trees and stones, which appeared to her like mountains, she finally reached the door of the hive, just when cold drops of rain were beginning to fall.

"Oh!, my God!" exclaimed the forsaken bee. "It's going to rain, and I'm going to die from the cold."

And she attempted to enter the hive.

But again they did not let her in.

"Forgive me!" cried the bee. "Let me come in."

"It's too late" they answered.

"Please, sister bees! I'm sleepy."

"It's later still."

"Friends, have mercy! I'm cold!"

"Impossible."

"For the last time! I'm going to die!"

Then they said:

"No, you will not die. You will learn in a single night what well deserved rest from having worked hard is like. Go away."

And they cast her out.

And so, trembling with cold, her wings wet and stumbling along, the bee dragged herself until she suddenly rolled down into a hole; or rather, fell rolling to the bottom of a cavern.

She thought she would never stop falling. At last she reached the bottom, and suddenly found herself in front of a green snake with a brick-red colored back, which was watching her coiled and ready to pounce on her.

Actually, that cave was the hollow of a tree that had been transplanted some time ago, and which the snake had chosen as its den.

Snakes eat bees, which they like very much. So the bee, finding herself in front of its enemy, closed her eyes and muttered:

"Farewell, dear life! Surely this is my final hour."

But to her great surprise, the snake did not devour her, but instead said to her:

"How are you doing, little bee? You must not be too much of a hard worker to be here at this hour."

"It's true," muttered the bee. "I don't work and its all my fault."

"That being the case," added the snake mockingly "I'm going to rid the world of such a bad bug as yourself. I'm going to eat you, bee."

Trembling, the bee then said:

—¡No es justo, eso, no es justo! No es justo que usted me coma porque es más fuerte que yo. Los hombres saben lo que es justicia.

—¡Ah, ah! —exclamó la culebra, enroscándose ligero— ¿Tú conoces bien a los hombres? ¿Tú crees que los hombres, que les quitan la miel a ustedes, son más justos, grandísima tonta?

—No es por eso que nos quitan la miel —respondió la abeja.

—¿Y por qué, entonces?

—Porque son más inteligentes.

Así dijo la abejita. Pero la culebra se echó a reír exclamando:

—¡Bueno! Con justicia o sin ella, te voy a comer; apróntate.

Y se echó atrás, para lanzarse sobre la abeja. Pero ésta exclamó:

—Usted hace eso porque es menos inteligente que yo.

—¿Yo, menos inteligente que tú, mocosa? —se río la culebra.

—Así es —afirmó la abeja.

—Pues bien —dijo la culebra, vamos a verlo. Vamos a hacer dos pruebas. El que haga la prueba más rara, ése gana. Si gano yo, te como.

—¿Y si gano yo? —Preguntó la abeja.

—Si ganas tú —repuso la enemiga, tienes el derecho de pasar la noche aquí, hasta que sea de día. ¿Te conviene?

—Aceptado —contestó la abeja.

La culebra se echó a reír de nuevo, porque se le había ocurrido una cosa que jamás podría una abeja. Y he aquí lo que hizo:

Salió un instante afuera, tan velozmente que la abeja no tuvo tiempo de nada. Y volvió trayendo una cápsula de semillas de eucalipto, de un eucalipto que estaba al lado de la colmena y que le daba sombra.

Los muchachos hacen bailar como trompos esas cápsulas, y los llaman trompitos de eucalipto.

—Esto es lo que voy a hacer —dijo la culebra. —¡Fíjate bien, atención!

Y arrollando vivamente la cola alrededor del trompito como un piolín, la desenvolvió a toda velocidad, con tanta rapidez que el trompito quedó bailando y zumbando como un loco.

La culebra se reía, y con mucha razón, porque jamás una abeja ha hecho ni podrá bailar un trompito.

THE LAZY BEE

"It's not fair, it's just not fair. It's not fair that you can eat me just because you're stronger than I am. Men know all about justice."

"Oh, oh!" exclaimed the snake, quickly coiling herself up. "You think you know men? You believe that man, who takes away honey from you, is more just, you great big fool."

"That's not the reason they take our honey away" replied the bee.

"What's the reason, then?"

"They are more intelligent."

So spoke the little bee. But the snake burst out laughing and exclaimed:

"Be it as it may, just or not, I'm going to eat you, so get ready."

And it flung itself back, ready to pounce on the bee. But the bee exclaimed:

"You're doing that because you are less intelligent than I am", declared the bee.

"I, less intelligent than you, you little brat?" The snake laughed.

"Exactly," declared the bee.

"Well, we'll see if this is the case. We'll do a couple of tests. The one who performs the most ingenious stunt will be the winner. If I win, I get to eat you."

"And if I win?" the little bee asked.

"If you win replied the enemy, you get to spend the night here, till daybreak. Does this arrangement suit you?"

"Agreed" answered the bee.

The snake took to laughing again, because she had thought of something that no bee could ever do. And this is what she did:

She went outside for an instant, so swiftly that the bee had no time to do anything. And she returned carrying a pod filled with eucalyptus seeds, from a eucalyptus tree next to the hive and which provided it with shade.

Youngsters make these pods whirl like spinning tops, and they call them eucalyptus spinning tops.

"This is what I'm going to do," said the snake. Look and pay attention."

And rolling up her tail briskly around the little spinning top as if it were string, she unrolled it at such speed that the small spinning top just stayed there spinning and humming like crazy.

The snake was laughing, and with good reason, because no bee has ever been, nor will ever be able to make a spinning top spin.

Pero cuando el trompito, que se había quedado dormido zumbando, como les pasa a los trompos de naranjo, cayó por fin al suelo, la abeja dijo:

—Esa prueba es muy linda, y yo nunca podré hacer eso.

—Entonces, te como —exclamó la culebra.

—¡Un momento! Yo no puedo hacer eso; pero hago una cosa que nadie hace.

—¿Qué es eso?

—¡Desaparecer!

—¿Cómo? —exclamó la culebra dando un salto de sorpresa—. ¿Desaparecer sin salir de aquí?

—Sin salir de aquí.

—¿Y sin esconderte en la tierra?

—Sin esconderme en la tierra.

—¡Pues bien, hazlo! Y si no lo haces, te como en seguida —Dijo la culebra.

El caso es que mientras el trompito bailaba, la abeja había tenido tiempo de examinar la caverna, y había visto una plantita que crecía allí. Era un arbustillo, casi un yuyito, con grandes hojas del tamaño de una moneda de dos centavos.

La abeja se arrimó a la plantita, teniendo cuidado de no tocarla, y dijo así:

—Ahora me toca a mí, señora Culebra. Me va a hacer el favor de darse vuelta, y contar hasta tres. Cuando diga "tres", búsqueme por todas partes ¡ya no estaré más!

Y así pasó, en efecto. La culebra dijo rápidamente: "uno..., dos..., tres..., y se volvió y abrió la boca cuan grande era, de sorpresa: allí no había nadie. Miró arriba, abajo, a todos lados, recorrió los rincones, la plantita, tanteó todo con su lengua. Inútil: la abeja había desaparecido.

La culebra comprendió entonces que si su prueba del trompito era muy buena, la prueba de la abeja era simplemente extraordinaria. ¿Qué se había hecho? ¿Dónde estaba?

No había modo de hallarla.

—¡Bueno! —exclamó por fin—. Me doy por vencida. ¿Dónde estás?

Una voz que apenas se oía —la voz de la abejita— salió del medio de la cueva.

But when the little top stopped spinning and humming along and finally fell to the ground –as eventually happens to all spinning tops– the bee said:

"That's a very neat trick, and I'll never be able to do that".

"Then, I get to eat you" exclaimed the snake.

"Just a moment! I can't do that; but I'll do something no one else can do."

"What's that?"

"Disappear!"

"How?" exclaimed the snake giving a startled jump in surprise. "Disappear without leaving here?"

"Without leaving here."

"And without your hiding in the earth?"

"Without my hiding in the earth."

"All right, do it! And if you don't do it, I'll eat you right away" said the snake.

The thing is that while the little spinning top was spinning, the bee had time to examine the cavern, and had seen a small plant that grew there. It was a little shrub, almost a weed with large leaves the size of a two-cent coin.

The bee got close to the little plant, being careful not to touch it, and spoke as follows:

"Now it's my turn, Mrs. Snake. You will do me the favor of turning around, and counting to three. When you say "three", look for me everywhere. I will not be here any longer!"

And that, as a matter of fact, is what happened. The snake said rapidly: "one..., two..., three...", and turned around and, struck with surprise, opened her mouth as wide as it would open: there was no one there. She looked above, below, on all sides, inspected all the corners, the little plant, felt everything with her tongue. Everything proved futile: the bee had disappeared.

The snake realized that if the trick of the little spinning top was clever, the bee's trick was simply extraordinary. What had happened to her? Where was she?

There was no way of finding her.

"All right," she exclaimed at last. "I give up. Where are you?"

A voice that could barely be heard –the voice of the little bee– came out from the middle of the cave.

–¿No me vas a hacer nada? –dijo la voz. –¿Puedo contar con tu juramento?

–Sí –respondió la culebra. –Te lo juro. ¿Dónde estás?

–Aquí –respondió la abejita, apareciendo súbitamente de entre una hoja cerrada de la plantita.

¿Qué había pasado? Una cosa sencilla: la plantita en cuestión era muy sensitiva, muy común también en Buenos Aires, y que tiene la particularidad de que sus hojas se cierran al menor contacto. Solamente que esta aventura pasaba en Misiones, donde la vegetación es muy rica, y por lo tanto muy grandes las hojas de las sensitivas. De aquí que al contacto de la abeja, las hojas se cerraran, ocultando completamente al insecto.

La inteligencia de la culebra no había alcanzado nunca darse cuenta de ese fenómeno; pero la abeja lo había observado, y se aprovecha de él para salvar su vida.

La culebra no dijo nada, pero quedó muy irritada con su derrota, tanto que la abeja pasó toda la noche recordando a su enemiga la promesa que había hecha de respetarla.

Fue una noche larga, interminable, que las dos pasaron arrimadas contra la pared más alta de la caverna, porque la tormenta se había desencadenado y el agua entraba como un río adentro.

Hacía mucho frío, además, y adentro reinaba la oscuridad más completa. De cuando en cuando, la culebra sentía impulsos de lanzarse sobre la abeja, y ésta creía entonces llegado el término de su vida.

Nunca, jamás, creyó la abejita que una noche podría ser tan fría, tan larga, tan horrible. Recordaba su vida anterior, durmiendo noche tras noche en la colmena bien calentita, y lloraba entonces en silencio.

Cuando llego el día, y salió el sol, porque el tiempo se había mejorado, la abejita voló y lloró otra vez en silencio ante la puerta de la colmena hecha por el esfuerzo de la familia.

Las abejas de guardia la dejaron pasar sin decir nada, porque comprendieron que la que volvía no era la paseandera haragana, sino una abeja que había hecho en sólo una noche un duro aprendizaje de la vida.

Así fue, en efecto. En adelante, ninguna como ella recogió tanto polen ni fabricó tanta miel. Y cuando el otoño llegó, y llegó

"You're not going to do anything to me are you?" said the voice. "Can I count on your promise?"

"Yes" replied the snake. "I promise you. Where are you?"

"Here" replied the little bee, appearing unexpectedly from inside a closed leaf of the little plant.

What had happened? Something quite simple. The little plant in question, very common here in Buenos Aires, was very sensitive and had the peculiarity of closing its leaves at the least bit of contact. Except that this adventure takes place in Misiones where the vegetation is quite fertile, and therefore the leaves of this type of plant are very large. And this is why when the bee made contact with the leaves, they closed, thus completely hiding the insect.

The snake had never been intelligent enough to perceive this phenomena; but the bee had noticed it, and took advantage of it to save her life.

The snake did not say anything, but she felt quite irritated on account of her defeat, so much so that the bee spent all night reminding her enemy of the promise she made to keep her word.

It was a seemingly endless night that both spent leaning against the tallest wall of the cavern, because the storm had broken out and the water was entering inside like a river.

It was also very cold, and inside complete darkness prevailed.

From time to time, the snake felt a certain impulse to pounce on the bee, and each time this happened the bee believed that her life was coming to an end.

Never, ever did the little bee think that just one night could be so cold, so long, so horrible. She recalled her former life, sleeping night after night in the hive nice and warm, and then she would begin to cry in silence.

When daybreak came and the sun came out, because the weather had cleared, the little bee flew off and again cried silently upon reaching the door of the hive, built through the effort of the entire bee family.

The bees on duty let her come through without saying anything, because they understood that the bee that was coming back was not the same lazy gadabout, but rather one that in a single night had learned a harsh lesson about life.

And, as a matter of fact, that's the way it turned out. Henceforth, no one gathered as much pollen nor produced as much honey as she

también el término de sus días, tuvo aún tiempo de dar una última lección antes de morir a las jóvenes abejas que la rodeaban:

–No es nuestra inteligencia, sino nuestro trabajo que nos hace fuertes. Yo usé una sola vez de mi inteligencia, y fue para salvar mi vida. No habría necesitado de ese esfuerzo, si hubiera trabajado como todas. Me he cansado tanto volando de aquí para allá, como trabajando. Lo que me faltaba era la noción del deber, que adquirí aquella noche.

–Trabajen, compañeras, pensando que el fin a que tienden nuestros esfuerzos –la felicidad de todos– es muy superior a la fatiga de cada uno. A esto los hombres llaman ideal, y tienen razón. No hay otra filosofía en la vida de un hombre y de una abeja.

❖

did. And when fall arrived, and the last of her days were coming to an end, she still had time to give to the other young bees that surrounded her one last lesson before dying:

"It's not our intelligence, but rather our work that makes us strong. I made use of my intelligence just once, and that was to save my life. I would not have had need of that effort, had I worked like all the others. I tired myself flying from one place to another as much as if I had worked. What I lacked was the notion of duty, which I acquired that night.

"I urge you to work, my fellow-workers, keeping in mind that the end result –everyone's happiness– is far more important than individual hardship. Men call this an ideal, and rightly so. There can be no other philosophy of life, either in man or in bees."

❖

Gutiérrez Nájera
(México 1859-1895)

The transition from Romantism to Moder-
nism in Latin American produced a very
interesting hybrid, of which this story is a
fitting example. The romantics of old
sought refuge in the esthetics of the new
movement, became cosmopolitan, aristo-
cratic, sophisticated. Led by Ruben Dario,
the innovator of the new movement, the
modernists gradually replaced introspec-
tion for visual representation. Although *A
Sad Tale* is still undeniably romantic, there
are various elements in the story pointing
to a new direction in the quest for capturing the illusive ideal of Beauty in art and
literature. Although written in Mexico, the
narrative could very well take place in
Paris, Rome or Vienna. We have included
this particular story for its literary signifi-
cance in the evolution of the Latin American short story.

CUENTO TRISTE

Por Manuel Gutiérrez Nájera

Por qué me pides versos? Hace ya tiempo que mi pobre imaginación, como una flor cortada demasiado temprano, quedó en las tinieblas, tan oscura como la noche y como mi alma. ¿Por qué me pides versos? Tu sabes bien que del laúd sin cuerdas no brotan armonías y que del nido abandonado ya no brotan gorjeos. Vino el invierno y desnudó los árboles; se helaron las aguas del río donde bañabas tu pie breve y aquella casa, oculta entre los fresnos, ha oído frases de amor que no pronunciaron nuestros labios y risas que no alegraban nuestras almas. Parece que un amor inmenso nos separa.

Yo he corrido tras el amor y tras la gloria, como van los niños tras la coqueta mariposa que se burla de la persecución y de sus gritos.

Todas las rosas que encontré tenían espinas, y todos los corazones olvido.

El libro de mi vida tiene una sola página de felicidad, y ésa es la tuya.

No me pidas versos. Mi alma es como esos pájaros viejos que no saben cantar y pierden sus plumas una a una, cuando sopla el cierzo de diciembre.

Hubo un momento que yo creí que el amor era absoluto y único. No hay más que un amor en mi alma, como no hay más que un sol en el cielo, como decía entonces. Después supe, estudiando astronomía que los soles son muchos.

Toqué a la puerta de muchos corazones y no me abrieron porque dentro no había nadie.

A SAD TALE

By Manuel Gutiérrez Nájera

W hy do you ask poems of me? It has been a while now that my poor imagination, like a flower cut prematurely, has remained in a gloom as dark as the night and dark as my soul. Why do you ask poems of me? As you well know a lyre without strings brings forth no harmony, nor can any warbling sprout forth from an abandoned nest. Winter came and stripped the trees; the water where you used to bathe your foot ever so daintily is now frozen, and that house hidden amongst the ash trees has heard phrases of love our lips never uttered and laughter our happy hearts never inspired. An immense love seems to separates us.

I have chased after love and after glory, like children chase after the coquettish butterfly that makes fun of its persecution and of their cries.

All the roses I found had thorns, and all hearts were unfaithful.

The book of my life has a single page of happiness, and that page belongs to you.

Do not ask me for poetry. My soul is like that of older birds that can no longer sing, and who, when December's North wind blows, loose their feathers one by one.

There was a moment when I believed that love was absolute and unique. There is only one love in my soul, just as there is only one sun in the sky, as I used to say. Then I learned, while studying astronomy, that there are many suns.

I knocked at the door of many hearts but since there was no one inside, no one ever opened.

CUENTO TRISTE

Yo vuelvo ya de todos los países azules en que florecen las naranjas de color de oro. Estoy enfermo y triste. No creo más que en Dios, en mis padres y en tí. No me pidas versos.

Preciso es, sin embargo, que te hable y te cuente una por una mis tristezas. Por eso voy a escribirte, para que leas mis pobres cartas junto a tu ventana, y pienses en el ausente que jamás ha de volver. Las golondrinas vuelven después de larga ausencia, y se refugian en las ramas del pino. La brújula señala siempre el Norte. Mi corazón te busca a tí.

¿De qué quieres que te hable? Deja afuera la obscuridad y haz que iluminen tu alma las claridades del amor. Somos dos islas separadas por el mar; pero los vientos llevan a tí mis palabras y yo adivino las tuyas. Cuando la tarde caiga y las estrellas comienzan a brillar en el espacio, abre tú los pliegues cerrados que te envío, y escucha las ardientes frases de pasión que lleva el aire a tus oídos. Figúrate que estamos solos en el bosque; que olvidé todo el daño que me has hecho, y que en el fondo del cupé capitoneado te hablo de mis ambiciones y de mis sueños. Oyeme como escuchas el canto de las aves, el rumor de las aguas, el susurro de la brisa. Hablemos ambos de las cosas frívolas, esto es, de las cosas serias. La tarde va a morir; el viento mueve apenas sus alas como un pájaro cansado; los caballos que tiran del carruaje corren hacia la casa en busca de descanso; la sombra va cayendo lentamente... aprovechemos los instantes.

Hace muy pocos días paseaba yo por el parque pensando en tí. La tarde estaba nublada y mi corazón triste.

¡Cómo han cambiado las cosas! Los carruajes que van hoy al paseo no son los mismos que tú y yo veíamos. Veo caras nuevas tras los cristales y no encuentro las que antes distinguía. ¿Te acuerdas de aquella que encontrábamos siempre en *trois quart* a la entrada del paseo? Pues voy a referirte su novela. Amaba mucho; las ilusiones cantaban en su alma como una bandada de ruiseñores; se casó y la engañaron. Todavía recuerdo la impaciencia con que contaba los días que faltaban para su matrimonio. La noche que recibió el traje de novia creyó volverse loca de contenta. Yo la miré en

A SAD TALE

I now return from countries under whose blue skies golden oranges bloom. I am ill and sad. I believe only in God, my parents and you. Don't ask poems of me.

It is necessary, however, that I speak to you and relate, one by one, my feelings of sadness. That is why I will write to you, so that you'll read my poor letters next to your window, that you might think of the one who cannot be present now, and who will never return. The swallows always return after a long absence, and take refuge in the pine branches. The compass needle always points North. My heart searches for you.

What do you wish me to talk about? Leave the darkness outside and let the glow of love illuminate your soul. We are two islands separated by the sea; but the winds carry forth my words to you and I can guess yours. At nightfall when the stars begin to shine in the heavens, open the sealed letters that I send you, and listen to the ardent phrases of passion that the wind carries to your ears. Just imagine that we are alone in the forest; that I have forgiven all the hurt that you have caused me, and that from the back seat of an upholstered carriage I speak to you of my ambitions and my dreams. Listen to me in the same way that you listen to the singing of birds, the murmur of water, the gentle sea breeze. Let us both speak of frivolous things, that is, of serious things. The evening is coming to a close; the wind like a tired bird barely moves it wings; the horses pulling the carriage hastily head for home in search of rest; night is falling ever so slowly... let us take advantage of these moments.

Just a few days ago I was strolling through the park thinking of you. It was a cloudy afternoon and my heart was sad.

How things have changed! The carriages which now stroll by are not the same as those you and I used to see. I see new faces behind the windows and cannot find those I once recognized. Do you remember the lady that we always used to find in a three-quarter length coat at the entrance of the promenade? Well let me tell you her story.

She was deeply in love; her dreams sang in her soul like a flock of nightingales; she married and was deceived. I can still remember the impatience with which she counted the days left for her marriage. The night she received her wedding dress she was so happy she thought she would go mad. I saw her on the following day at

la iglesia el día siguiente, coronada de blancos azahares, trémula de emoción y con los ojos henchidos de lágrimas. ¡Quién hubiera dicho que aquel matrimonio era una entierro? Se amaban mucho los dos, o, por lo menos, lo decían así. Iban a realizar sus ilusiones; la riqueza les preparó un palacio espléndido y los que de pie en la playa la miramos partir en un barco de oro, dijimos: ¡Dios la lleva con felicidad!

Unos meses después encontré a su marido en un café.

—¿Y Blanca?

—¡Está algo mala!

Era verdad, Blanca estaba mala; Blanca se moría. Enrique la dejaba por ir en pos de los placeres fáciles, y Blanca, sola en su pequeña habitación, pasaba las noches sin dormir, mirando cómo se persiguen y se juntan las agujas en la muestra del reloj. Una noche Enrique no volvió. Al día siguiente, Blanca estaba más pálida: parecía de cera.

Se hubiera creído que la luz del alba, que Blanca vio aparecer muchas veces desde su balcón, le había teñido el rostro con sus colores de azucena.

—¿Por qué no viene? —preguntaba, sondeando con los ojos la obscuridad profunda de la calle.

Y graznaban las lechuzas, y el aire frío de la mañana le hería el rostro, y Enrique no volvía. De repente suenan pasos en las baldosas. Blanca se inclina sobre el barandal para ver si venía. ¡Esperanza frustrada! Era un borracho que regresaba a su casa, tropezando con los faroles y las puertas.

Así pasaron días, semanas, meses; Blanca cada día estaba peor. Los médicos no atinaban la cura de su enfermedad. ¿Acaso hay médicos del alma? Una noche Blanca le dijo a Enrique:

—No te vayas. Creo que voy a morirme. No me dejes.

Enrique se rió de sus temores y fue al círculo, donde le esperaban sus amigos. ¿Quién se muere a los veinte años!

Blanca lo vio partir con tristeza. Se puso después delante de un espejo, alisó sus cabellos y comenzó a prender entre sus rizos diminutos botones de azahar.

Dos grande círculos morados rodeaban sus ojos. Llamó en seguida a su camarera, su puso el traje blanco que le había servido

church crowned with a wreath of orange blossoms, trembling with emotion and her eyes swollen with tears. Who would have said that their marriage was to be a funeral? The two loved each other very much, or, at least, that was what everyone said. Their dreams were about to come true; their wealth provided them with a splendid palace and those of us standing at the edge of the seashore who saw her leave in a golden boat, said: God is leading her to happiness!

A few months later I met up with her husband in a cafe.

"How is Blanca?"

"She's somewhat ill."

It was true. Blanca was ill; she was dying. Enrique would leave her alone in search of easy pleasures and Blanca, by herself in her small bedroom, would spend her nights awake, looking at how the hands on the face of the clock followed and joined each other. One night, Enrique did not return. On the following day, Blanca was even more pale; she looked like a wax figure.

One would have thought that the dawn's light, which Blanca had seen appear so many times from her balcony, had tinged her face with the colors of a water lily.

"Why doesn't he come?," she would ask, probing with her eyes the profound obscurity of the street.

The owls were whooing and she could feel the cold early morning air on her face, and Enrique still had not come back. Suddenly there was the sound of footsteps on the tiled floor. Blanca leaned over the handrail to see if he was coming. It was false hope! It was a drunkard returning home, tripping along the way against streetlamps and doors.

Days passed, then weeks, then months: each day that went by, Blanca would get worse. Her doctors simply could not find the source of her illness. Are there doctors of the soul, by chance?

One night, Blanca said to Enrique:

"Don't leave me. I think I am going to die."

Enrique laughed at her fears and went off to his club, where his friends awaited him. Who dies at twenty years of age?

Blanca saw him leave with sadness. Then she went to a mirror and smoothed her hair and began placing orange blossom buds between her diminutive curls.

Two large dark circles surrounded her eyes. She immediately summoned her chambermaid, put on the white dress used on her

para el día del matrimonio y se acostó. Al amanecer, cuando Enrique volvió a su casa, vio abiertos los balcones de su alcoba; cuatro cirios ardían en torno de la cama. Blanca estaba muerta.

—¿Ya lo ves? La vida mundana, tan brillante por fuera, es como los sepulcros blanqueados de que nos habla el Evangelio. La riqueza oculta con su manto de arlequín muchas miserias.

Cierra tus oídos a las palabras del eterno tentador. No ambiciones el oro, que es tan frío como el corazón de una coqueta. Sé buena, reza mucho y ama poco.

❖

wedding day and went to bed. At dawn, when Enrique returned home, he could see that the balcony windows to his bedroom were open; four candles were burning next to the bed. Blanca was dead.

"Do you see now?" Worldly life, so brilliant on the outside, is like the whitewashed sepulchres of which the Gospel speaks. Wealth hides with its Harlequin mantle a great number of miseries.

Close your ears to the words of the Devil. Do not seek after gold, for it is as cold as the heart of a frivolous girl. Be good, pray ardently and love little.

❖

Leopoldo Lugones
(Argentina. 1874-1938)

Leopoldo Lugones' literary merit much
like that of Jorge Luis Borges lies in his
originality. What these writers lack in in-
tenseness, warmth and intimacy they
make up in imagination, inventiveness and
ingenuity. Both are born storytellers drawing from their vast background of cultural
and scientific knowledge to weave stories
in which the fantastic is made to appear
very real, and the real highly fantastic. The
wealth of apparent documentation and the
methodical aspects of the experiment
which is related in the story reveals
Lugones as a master of his craft. The story,
in fact, seemed more a documentary than
a narration per se. It is to Lugones' merit
that he is able to cleverly present an openly
outlandish fantasy -that is, an attempt to
make a monkey speak- and treat it in the
most serious and seemingly scientific
manner.

YZUR

Por Leopoldo Lugones

Compré el mono en el remate de un circo que había quebrado. La primera vez que se me ocurrió tentar la experiencia a cuyo relato están dedicadas estas líneas fue una tarde, leyendo no sé dónde que los naturales de Java atribuían la falta de lenguaje articulado en los monos a abstención, no a la incapacidad. "No hablan, decían, para que no los hagan trabajar."

Semejante idea, nada profundo al principio, acabó por preocuparme hasta convertirse en este postulado antropológico: los monos fueron hombres que por una razón u otra dejaron de hablar. El hecho produjo la atrofia de sus órganos de fonación y de los centros cerebrales del lenguaje; debilitó casi hasta suprimirla la relación entre unos y otros, el idioma de la especie en el grito inarticulado, y el humano primitivo descendió a ser animal.

Claro está que si llegara a demostrarse esto quedarían explicadas desde luego todas las anomalías que hacen del mono un ser tan singular; pero ello no tendrían sino una demostración posible: volver el mono al lenguaje.

Entre tanto había corrido el mundo con el mío, vinculándolo cada vez más por medio de peripecias y aventuras. En Europa llamó la atención y, de haberlo querido, llegó a darle la celebridad de un *Consul**, pero mi seriedad de hombre de negocios mal se avenía con tales payasadas.

Trabajado por mi idea fija del lenguaje de los monos, agoté

---

* *Consul*: nombre de un mono célebre hacía comienzos del siglo.

YZUR: A MONKEY'S LAMENT

By Leopoldo Lugones

I purchased the monkey at the close-out sale of a circus which had gone out of business. It first occurred to me to undertake the experiment whose narrative these lines are devoted to, one afternoon, while reading, I do not recall where, that the natives of Java attributed the lack of articulated language in monkeys to abstention rather than inability. "They don't speak, they said, so that they will not be made to work."

Such an idea, not at all profound in the beginning, ended up preoccupying me to such an extent that it turned into the following anthropological axiom: monkeys were once human beings that for one reason or another ceased speaking. This occurrence produced an atrophy in the organs of vocalization and in the cerebral centers of speech, weakening almost to the point of suppression, the relationship between one and the other. The language of that species then became an inarticulate shriek, and primitive humankind reverted to an animal state.

Of course, if this could be established, all the anomalies that make the monkey such a singular being would then be explained; but there could only be one way to determine the validity of this theory: have the monkey speak again.

Meanwhile I had travelled all over the world with mine, and through a series of adventures and feats he became increasingly famous. In Europe he attracted a great deal of attention, and could have reached the celebrity status of another *Consul**; but my sense of responsibility as a business man was not in keeping with such foolishness.

Taken up with my set idea regarding the language of monkeys,

---

* *Consul*: name of a monkey who became famous at the beginning of this century.

toda la bibliografía concerniente al problema, sin ningún resultado apreciable. Sabía únicamente, con entera seguridad, *que no hay razón científica para que el mono no hable.* Esto llevaba cinco años de meditaciones.

Yzur (nombre cuyo origen nunca pude descubrir, pues lo ignoraba igualmente su anterior patrón), Yzur era ciertamente un animal notable. La educación del circo, bien que reducida casi enteramente al mimetismo, había desarrollado mucho sus facultades; y eso era lo que me incitaba a ensayar sobre él mi en apariencia disparatada teoría.

Por otra parte, se sabía que el chimpancé (Yzur lo era) es entre los monos el mejor provisto de cerebro y uno de los más dóciles, lo cual aumentaba mis probabilidades. Cada vez que lo veía avanzar en dos pies, con las manos a la espalda para conservar el equilibrio, y su aspecto de marinero borracho, la convicción de su humanidad detenida se vigorizaba en mí.

No hay a la verdad razón alguna para que el mono no articule absolutamente. Su lenguaje natural, es decir el conjunto de gritos con que se comunica a sus semejantes, es asaz variado; su laringe, por más distinta que resulte de la humana, nunca lo es tanto como la del loro, que habla, sin embargo; y en cuanto a su cerebro, fuera de que la comparación con el de este último animal desvanece toda duda, basta recordar que el del idiota es también rudimentario, a pesar de lo cual hay cretinos que pronuncian algunas palabras. Por lo que hace a la circunvolución de Broca*, depende, es claro, del desarrollo total del cerebro; fuera de que no está probado que ella sea fatalmente el sitio de localización del lenguaje. Si es el caso de localización mejor establecido en anatomía, los hechos contradictorios son desde luego incontestables.

Felizmente, los monos tienen, entre sus muchas malas condiciones, el gusto por aprender, como lo demuestra su tendencia imitativa; la memoria feliz, la reflexión que llega hasta una profunda facultad de disimulo, y la atención comparativamente más desarrollada que en el niño. Es, pues, un sujeto pedagógico de los más favorables.

Circunvolución de Broca: situada en el lóbulo frontal izquierdo del cerebro; en ella se localiza el centro del lenguaje articulado.

YZUR: A MONKEY'S LAMENT

I exhausted all bibliographies pertaining to this problem, without any appreciable result. I only knew, with complete certainty, that *there is no known scientific reason for monkeys not to speak.* This conclusion covered five years worth of meditation.

Yzur (a name whose origin I was never able to discover, since even the previous owner was ignorant of it), Yzur was certainly an exceptional animal. The education he received in the circus, although almost confined to mimicry, had greatly developed his faculties; and this was what encouraged me even more to test on him my seemingly foolish theory.

On the other hand, it is known that chipanzees (Yzur was one) are endowed with one of the most highly developed brains among monkeys and is one of the most docile of creatures, something which increased my probabilities. Each time I saw him advancing on his two feet, with his hand toward the back to help balance himself, and with his demeanor of a drunken sailor, the conviction of his thwarted humanity grew stronger within me.

There is really no good reason why monkeys should not speak. Its natural language, that is, the series of screams with which it communicates with its own kind is rather varied; their larynx, however different from the human one, is never quite as different as that of parrots, who nonetheless do speak; and with respect to their brain, aside from the fact that this comparison with the latter animal dispels all doubt, one needs only to recall that the idiot's brain is also rudimentary, despite the fact that there are cretins who are able to pronounce some words. With respect to the Broca Circumvolution*, the location depends, of course, on the full development of the brain; outside of the fact that it has not been proven that this is inevitably the region where language is located. Albeit the theory most widely accepted in anatomy, the facts to the contrary are nevertheless indisputable.

Fortunately, monkeys have, along with a great lack of ability, a fondness for learning, as can be seen from their tendency towards imitation; good memory, a degree of reflection which can reach a high degree of craftiness, and an attentiveness comparatively more developed than that of a child. It is, therefore, a most favorable pedagogical subject.

The Broca Circumvolution: Located in the left frontal lobe of the brain, which serves as the center of articulated speech.

El mío era joven además, y es sabido que la juventud constituye la época más intelectual del mono. La dificultad estriba solamente en el método que emplearía para comunicarle la palabra. Conocía todas las infructuosas tentativas de mis antecesores; y está de más decir que, ante la competencia de algunos de ellos y la nulidad de todos sus esfuerzos, mis propósitos fallaron más de una vez; cuando el tanto pensar sobre aquel tema fue llevándome a esta conclusión:

Lo primero consiste en desarrollar el aparato de fonación del mono.

Así es, en efecto, como se procede con los sordomudos antes de llevarlos a la articulación; y no bien hube reflexionado sobre esto, cuando las analogías entre el sordomudo y el mono se agolparon en mi espíritu.

Primero de todo, su extraordinario movilidad mímica que compensa al lenguaje articulado, demostrando que no por dejar de hablar se deja de pensar, así haya disminución de esta facultad por la paralización de aquélla. Después, otros caracteres más peculiares por ser más específicos: la diligencia en el trabajo, la fidelidad, el coraje, aumentados hasta la certidumbre por estas dos condiciones cuya comunidad es verdaderamente reveladora: la facilidad para los ejercicios de equilibrio y la resistencia al mareo.

Decidí, entonces, empezar mi obra con una verdadera gimnasia de los labios y de la lengua de mi mono, tratándolo en esto como a un sordomudo. En lo restante, me favorecía el oído para establecer comunicaciones directas de palabra, sin necesidad de apelar al tacto. El lector verá que en esta parte prejuzgaba con demasiado optimismo.

Felizmente, el chimpancé es de todos los grandes monos el que tiene labios más movibles; y en el caso particular, habiendo padecido Yzur de anginas, sabía abrir la boca para que se la examinaran.

La primera inspección confirmó mis sospechas. La lengua permanecía en el fondo de su boca, como una masa inerte, sin otros movimientos que los de la deglución. La gimnasia produjo luego su efecto, pues a los dos meses ya sabía sacar la lengua para burlar. Esta fue la primera relación que conoció entre el movimiento de su

Besides, the one I had was young, and it is known that youth constitutes the most intellectual epoch of monkeys. The difficulty rested only in the method that I would use to communicate with him. I was aware of all the unsuccessful attempts of my predecessors; and it should be said that, mindful of the competence of some of them and the uselessness of their efforts, my own undertaking failed more than once; until constant reflection on the matter brought about the following conclusion:

The first step consists in developing the sound apparatus of the monkey.

That's the way, as a matter of fact, one proceeds with those who are deafmutes before teaching them articulation; and no sooner had I reflected on this, than the analogies between deafmutes and monkeys came vividly to mind.

First of all, the extraordinary mimical ability with which he compensates his lack of articulated language, demonstrates that not just because one stops talking does one stop thinking, even if there should be a lessening of the latter by the paralysis of the former. Additionally, other characteristics more peculiar for being more specific: diligence at work, loyalty, anger, strenghtened to a degree of conviction by these two conditions whose relationship is truly revealing: their sense of equilibrium and their resistance to dizziness.

I decided, therefore, to begin my task with a thorough training of the lips and tongue of my monkey, treating him in this aspect like a deafmute. As to the rest, I favored relying on the ear to establish direct oral communication, without the need to have recourse to the sense of touch. The reader will see that on this point I prejudged with too much optimism.

Fortunately, the chimpanzee is of all the great apes the one that has the most mobile lips; and in this particular case, since Yzur had once suffered from tonsillitis, he knew how to open his mouth so that it could be examined.

The first examination confirmed my suspicion. The tongue remained at the back of the mouth, like a lifeless mass, with no other movements other than those of swallowing. The exercise soon produced its effect, since in two month's time he knew how to stick his tongue out to make fun of people. This was the first relation-

lengua y una idea; una relación perfectamente acorde con su naturaleza, por otra parte.

Los labios dieron más trabajo, pues hasta hubo que estirárselos con pinzas; pero apreciaba –quizá por mi expresión– la importancia de aquella tarea anómala y la acometía con viveza. Mientras yo practicaba los movimientos labiales que debía imitar, permanecía sentado, rascándose la grupa con su brazo vuelto hacia atrás y guiñando en un concentración dubitativa, o alisándose las patillas con todo el aire de un hombre que armoniza sus ideas por medio de ademanes rítmicos. Al fin aprendió a mover los labios.

Pero el ejercicio del lenguaje es un arte difícil, como lo prueban los largos balbuceos del niño, que le llevan, paralelamente con su desarrollando intelectual, a la adquisición del hábito. Está demostrado, en efecto, que el centro propio de las inervaciones vocales se halla asociado con el de la palabra en forma tal, que el desarrollo normal de ambos depende de su ejercicios armónico; y eso lo había presentido en 1785 Heinicke, el inventor del método oral para la enseñanza de los sordomudos, como una consecuencia filosófica. Hablaba de una "concatenación dinámica de las ideas", frase cuya profunda claridad honraría a más de un psicólogo contemporáneo.

Yzur se encontraba, respecto al lenguaje, en la misma situación del niño que antes de hablar entiende ya muchas palabras; pero era mucho más apto para asociar los juicios que debía poseer sobre las cosas, por su mayor experiencia de la vida.

Estos juicios, que no debían ser sólo de impresión, sino también inquisitivos y disquisitivos, a juzgar por el carácter diferencial que asumían, lo cual supone un raciocinio abstracto, le daban un grado superior de inteligencia muy favorable por cierto a mi propósito.

Si mis teorías parecen demasiado audaces, basta con reflexionar que el silogismo, o sea, el argumento lógico fundamental, no es extraño a la mente de muchos animales. Como que el silogismo es originariamente una comparación entre dos sensaciones. Si no, ¿por qué los animales que conocen al hombre huyen de él, y no aquellos que nunca conocieron...?

Comencé, entonces, la educación fonética de Yzur.

ship he learned between the movement of the tongue and an idea: a relationship, moreover, in perfect harmony with his nature.

The lips presented a little more work, since it was even necessary to stretch them with pincers; but he realized –perhaps by my expression– the importance of such an anomalous task and the keenness with which I undertook it. While I practiced the lip movements he was to imitate, he remained seated, scratching his hindquarters with his arms turned toward his back and blinking with a perplexed look of concentration or smoothing his sideburns with all the air of a man that harmonizes his ideas by means of rhythmic gestures. Finally he learned to move his lips.

But the practice of language is a difficult art, as a child's long series of babbles proves, which leads him, parallel with its intellectual development, to the acquisition of the habit. It has been demonstrated, as a matter of fact, that the very center of the vocal nerves is found to be associated with that of the word in such a way, that the normal development of each depends on its harmonious exercise; and this had already been foreseen in 1785 by Heinecke, the creator of the oral method for the teaching of deafmutes, as a philosophical consequence. He spoke of a "dynamic-chain-of-ideas", a phrase whose profound clarity would honor more than one contemporary psychologist.

Yzur found himself, with respect to language, in the same situation of a child who before speaking understands many words beforehand ; but he was much more capable of associating judgments that he should possess over things, because of his greater experience in life.

These judgements, which should not be just of impression, but also of an inquisitive and highly exploratory nature, judging by the differential character they assumed, and which implies abstract reasoning, gave him a superior level of intelligence quite favorable in fact to my purpose.

If my theories seem to be a bit daring, one needs only to reflect that syllogism, or rather, the fundamental argument of logic, is not foreign to the mind of many animals. Since syllogism is originally a comparison between two sensations. If this is not the case, why is it then that animals that know humans shy away from them, but not from those that he has never known...?

I began, therefore, the phonetic education of Yzur.

Se trataba de enseñarle primero la palabra mecánica, para llevarlo progresivamente a la palabra sensata.

Poseyendo el mono la voz, es decir, llevando esto de ventaja al sordomudo, con más ciertas articulaciones rudimentarias, se trataba de enseñarle las modificaciones de aquélla, que constituyen los fonemas y su articulación, llamada por los maestros estática o dinámica, según que se refiera a las vocales o a las consonantes.

Dada la glotonería del mono, y siguiendo en esto un método empleado por Heinicke con los sordomudos, decidí asociar cada vocal con una golosina: *a* con papa; *e* con leche; *i* con vino; *o* con coco; *u* con azúcar, haciendo de modo que la vocal estuviese contenida en el nombre de la golosina, ora con dominio único y repetido de un solo sonido como en *papa*, *coco*, *leche*, ora reuniendo dos sonidos en en sola palabra como en *vino*, *azúcar*.

Todo anduvo bien mientras se trató de los vocales, o sea, los sonidos que se forman con la boca abierta. Yzur los aprendió en quince días. La *u* fue lo que más le costó pronunciar.

Las consonante le dieron un trabajo endemoniado; y a poco hube de comprender que nunca llegaría a pronunciar aquellas en cuya formación entra los dientes y las encías. Sus largos colmillos le estorbaban enteramente.

El vocabulario quedaba reducido, entonces, a las cinco vocales; la *b*, la *k*, la *m*, la *g*, la *f* y la *c*, es decir, todas aquellas consonantes en cuya formación no intervienen sino el paladar y la lengua.

Aun para esto no me bastó el oído. Hube de recurrir al tacto como con un sordomudo, apoyando su mano en mi pecho y luego en el suyo para que sintiera las vibraciones del sonido.

Y pasaron tres años sin conseguir que formara palabra alguna. Tendía a dar las cosas, como nombre propio, el de la letra cuyo sonido predominaba en ellas. Esto era todo.

En el circo había aprendido a ladrar, como los perros, sus compañeros de tareas; y cuando me veía desesperar ante las vanas tentativas para arrancarle la palabra, ladraba fuertemente como dándome todo lo que sabía. Pronunciaba aisladamente las vocales y las consonantes, pero no podía asociarlas. Cuando más, acertaba con una repetición vertiginosa de *pes* y de *emes*.

YZUR: A MONKEY'S LAMENT

It was a matter of first teaching him the mechanical word, and then gradually leading him on to the more meaningful word.

Since monkeys have a voice, that is to say, having this advantage over the deafmute along with better rudimentary articulations, it was a matter of teaching him the various voice variations, which constitute the phonemes and its articulation, called by teachers static or dynamic, according to whether they refer to vowels or consonants.

Given the gluttony of monkeys and following a method which takes this fact into account used by Heinicke with deafmutes, I decided to associate each vowel with one of his favorite foods or drinks; *a* with papa; *e* with leche; *i* with vino; *o* with coco; *u* with azúcar, making certain that the vowel was part of the name of the nourishment, at times limiting it to the basic sound repeated twice in the word like in *papa, coco, leche*, at times mixing the two sounds in individual words as in *vino, azúcar*.

All preceded well in respect to vowels, that is, those sounds made with an open mouth. Yzur learned them in fifteen days. The *u* was the one that gave him the most trouble.

The consonants gave him a heck of a time; and it did not take me long to understand that he would never be able to pronounce them whenever teeth and gums came into play. His long eyeteeth were totally in the way.

The vocabulary was therefore reduced to five vowels; the *b,* the *k*, the *m*, the *g,* the *f* and the *c*, that is, all those consonants in whose formation the palate and the tongue do not intervene.

Even then, the use of the ear alone was not sufficient. I had to resort to the sense of touch as with a deafmute, placing his hand on my chest and then on his so that he could feel the vibration of the sounds.

And so three years went by without his being able to form a single word. He had a tendency to assign to every object as proper name, that of the letter whose sound was prevalent in them. That was all.

In the circus he had learned how to bark, like the dogs he worked with. And when he would see me get discouraged in my unsuccessful attempts to get a word out of him, he barked loudly as if telling me all he knew. He uttered consonants and vowels independently, without being able to associate them. At best, he would repeat at lightning speed, a series of *p's* and *m's*.

Por despacio que fuera, se había operado un gran cambio en su carácter. Tenía menos movilidad en las facciones, la mirada más profunda, y adoptaba posturas meditabundas. Había adquirido, por ejemplo, la costumbre de contemplar las estrellas. Su sensibilidad se desarrollaba igualmente; se le iba notando una gran facilidad de lágrimas.

Las lecciones continuaban con inquebrantable tesón, aunque sin mayor éxito. Aquello había llegado a convertirse en una obsesión dolorosa, y poco a poco me sentía inclinado a emplear la fuerza. Mi carácter iba agriándose con el fracaso, hasta asumir una sorda animosidad contra Yzur. Este se intelectualizaba cada vez más, en el fondo de su mutismo rebelde, y empezaba a convencerme de que nunca lo sacaría de allí, cuando supe de golpe que no hablaba porque no quería.

El cocinero, horrorizado, vino a decirme una noche que había sorprendido al mono "hablando verdaderas palabras". Estaba, según su narración, acurrucado junto a una higuera de la huerta; pero el terror le impedía recordar lo esencial de esto, es decir, las palabras. Sólo creía retener dos: *cama* y *pipa*. Casi le doy de puntapiés por su imbecilidad.

No necesito decir que pasé la noche poseído de una gran emoción; y lo que en tres años no había cometido, el error que todo lo echó a perder, provino del enervamiento de aquel desvelo, tanto como mi excesiva curiosidad. En vez de dejar que el mono llegara naturalmente a la manifestación del lenguaje, lo llamé al día siguiente y procuré imponérselo por obediencia.

No conseguí sino las *pes* y las *emes* con que me tenía harto, las guiñadas hipócritas y –Dios me perdone– una cierta vislumbre de ironía en la azogada ubicuidad de sus muecas.

Me encolericé, y sin consideraciones alguna le di de azotes. Lo único que logré fue su llanto y un silencio absoluto que excluía hasta los gemidos.

A los tres días cayó enfermo, en una especie de sombría demencia complicada con síntomas de meningitis. Sanguijuelas, afusiones frías, purgantes, alcoholaturo de briona, bromuro: toda la terapéutica del espantoso mal le fue aplicada. Luché con desesperado brío, a impulsos de un remordimiento y de un temor. Aquél

However gradual, a great change had come about in his character. He had less mobility in his facial features, a deeper gaze, and was now adopting meditative postures. He had acquired, for example, the habit of contemplating the stars. His sensibility was also developing; one could also observe a great propensity to tears.

The lessons continued with unyielding persistence, although without much success. The whole thing had turned into a painful obsession, and I was beginning to feel inclined to using force. My character began to sour with my failure, to the point of turning into a suppressed animosity toward Yzur. He was becoming more intellectual, in the depths of his rebellious taciturnity, and I began to become convinced that I would not be able to get him out of this state, when all of a sudden I learned that if he did not speak, it was because he did not wish to.

Our cook, horrified, came and told me one night that he had surprised the monkey "speaking real words". He was, according to his story, curled up next to a fig tree in the orchard; but the terror of the moment prevented him from recalling the exact particulars, that is, the words. He thought he could remember only two of them: *cama* and *pipa*. I felt like kicking the heck out of him for his stupidity.

I need not point out that I spent the night possessed by a great excitement; and what I had not committed in three years, that is the error which spoiled everything, stemmed from nervous tension due to lack of sleep, as well as from excessive curiosity on my part. Instead of letting the monkey reach the speaking process in a natural way, I called out to him on the following day and tried to impose my will on him by way of obedience.

The only thing I managed to get from him was a bunch of *p*'s and *m*'s with which I was totally fed up, the hypocritical winks and – God forgive me– a glimmer of irony in his ever-present and agitated grimacing.

I became angry and without any consideration whatsoever I whipped him. The only thing I achieved was to make him wail and an absolute silence devoid even of moans.

Three days later he fell ill, with a type of melancholy dementia complicated with symptoms of meningitis; leeches, cold affusions, purgatives, a mixture of bryony alcohol, bromide: all the therapeutics for that dreadful illness was applied to him. I struggled with desperate vigor, propelled by remorse and fear. Remorse for believ-

por creer a la bestia una víctima de mi crueldad; éste por la suerte del secreto que quizá se llevaba a la tumba.

Mejoró al cabo de mucho tiempo, quedando, no obstante, tan débil, que no podía moverse de la cama. La proximidad de la muerte le había ennoblecido y humanizado. Sus ojos, llenos de gratitud, no se separaban de mí, siguiéndome por toda la habitación como dos bolas giratorias, aunque estuviese detrás de él; su mano buscaba las mías en una intimidad de convalecencia. En mi gran soledad, iba adquiriendo rápidamente la importancia de una persona.

El demonio del análisis, que no es sino una forma del espíritu de perversidad, me impulsaba, sin embargo, a renovar mis experiencias. En realidad, el mono había hablado. Aquello no podía quedar así.

Comencé muy despacio, pidiéndole las letras que sabía pronunciar. ¡Nada! Lo dejé solo durante horas, espiándolo por un agujerillo del tabique. ¡Nada! Le hablé con oraciones breves, procurando tocar su fidelidad o su glotonería. ¡Nada! Cuando aquellas eran patéticas, los ojos se le hinchaban de llanto. Cuando le decía una frase habitual , como el "yo soy tu amo" con que comenzaban todas mis lecciones, o el "tu eres mi mono" con que completaba mi anterior confirmación, para llevar a su espíritu la certidumbre de una verdad total, él asentía cerrando los párpado; pero no producía un sonido, ni siguiera llegaba a mover los labios.

Su convalecencia seguía estacionaria. La misma flacura, la misma tristeza. Era evidente que estaba enfermo de inteligencia y de dolor. Su unidad orgánica se había roto al impulso de una cerebración anormal, y día más, día menos, aquel era caso perdido.

Mas, a pesar de la mansedumbre que el progreso de la enfermedad aumentaba en él, su silencio, aquel desesperante silencio provocado por mi exasperación, no cedía. Desde un oscuro fondo de tradición petrificada en instinto, la raza imponía su milenario mutismo al animal, fortaleciéndose de voluntad atávica en las raíces mismas de su ser. Los antiguos hombres de la selva, que forzó el silencio, es decir, al suicidio intelectual, quién sabe qué bárbara injusticia, mantenían su secreto formado por misterios de bosques y abismos de prehistoria, en aquella decisión ya inconsciente, pero formidable con la inmensidad del tiempo.

ing the animal to be a victim of my cruelty; fear because of the particular secret that perhaps it was taking to the grave.

After a considerable period of time his health improved, remaining, however, so weak, that he could not move from his bed. The nearness of death had ennobled and humanized him. His eyes, filled with gratitude, never left me for a moment, following me all over the room like a pair of rotating spheres, even when I found myself behind him; his hand would seek mine with all the warmness of a convalescent. In my great solitude, as far as I was concerned, he was rapidly acquiring for me the importance of a person.

That evil thing called analysis, which is nothing more than the spirit of perversity, was inciting me, nevertheless, to renew my experiments. To be sure, the monkey had spoken. That no one could deny.

I started very slowly, asking of him the letters that he was able to utter. Nothing! I left him alone for several hours, spying on him through a small hole in the partition. Nothing! I spoke to him in brief phrases, trying to appeal to his loyalty or his gluttony. Nothing! When these were touching, his eyes would well up with tears. When I said a regular phrase, like "I am your master" with which I started all my lessons, or "You are my monkey" with which I would complete my aforementioned statement, in order for his spirit to recognize a complete truth, he would agree by closing his eyelids; but he would not produce a single sound, he would not even as much as move his lips.

His convalescence remained at a standstill. The same thinness, the same sadness. It was evident that he was sick from intellectual awareness and pain. His organic unity had broken down as a result of excessive thinking, and in a matter of days this would be a lost case.

But, despite the tameness which his worsening illness intensified, his silence, this infuriating silence caused by my exasperation, did not ease up. From an obscure past filled with traditions petrified into instinct, the race imposed its millennial silence on the animal, drawing strength from the atavistic roots of its own being. The ancient people of the jungle, which dictated that silence, that is, the intellectual suicide –who does not realize what a great injustice this was– kept their secret, shaped by the mysteries of the forest and the abysses of prehistory, by this then subconscious decision, but which was to become formidable with the immensity of time.

Infortunios del antropoide retrasado en la evolución cuya delantera tomaba el humano con un despotismo de sombría barbarie, había sin duda, destronado a las grandes familias cuadrumanas del dominio arbóreo de sus primitivos edenes, raleando sus filas, cautivando sus hembras para organizar la esclavitud desde el propio vientre materno, hasta infundir a su impotencia vencidas el acto de dignidad mortal que las llevaba a romper con el enemigo el vínculo superior también, pero infausto de la palabra, refugiándose como salvación suprema en la noche de la animalidad.

Y qué horrores, qué estupendas sevicias no habrían cometido los vencedores con la semibestia en trance de evolución, para que ésta, después de haber gustado el encanto espiritual que es el fruto paradisiático de las biblias, se resignara a aquella claudicación de su estirpe en la degradante igualdad de los inferiores; a aquel retroceso que cristalizaba por siempre su inteligencia en los gestos de una automatismo de acróbatas; a aquella gran cobardía de la vida que encorvaría eternamente, como en distintivo bestial, sus espaldas de dominado, imprimiéndole ese melancólico azoramiento que permanece en el fondo de su caricatura.

He aquí lo que al borde mismo del éxito había despertado mi malhumor en el fondo del limbo atávico. A través del millón de años, la palabra, con su conjuro, removía la antigua alma simiana; pero contra esa tentación que iba a violar las tinieblas de la animalidad protectora, la memoria ancestral, difundida en el especie bajo un instintivo horror, oponía también edad sobre edad como una muralla.

Yzur entró en agonía sin perder el conocimiento. Una dulce agonía a ojos cerrados, con respiración difícil, pulso vago, quietud absoluta, que sólo interrumpía para volver de cuando en cuando hacia mí, con una desgarrada expresión de eternidad, su cara de viejo triste. Y la última tarde, la tarde de su muerte, fue cuando ocurrió la cosa extraordinaria que me ha decidido a emprender esta narración.

Me había dormido a su cabecera, vencido por el calor y la quietud del crepúsculo que empezaba, cuando sentí de pronto que me asían por la muñeca.

Desperté sobresaltado. El mono, con los ojos muy abiertos, se moría definitivamente aquella vez, y su expresión era tan humana,

YZUR: A MONKEY'S LAMENT

The misfortunes of the anthropoid held back in their evolution and whose lead the human race took with a despotism of sullen barbarity, had, undoubtedly, dethroned the great four-footed families from the arboreal domination of its primitive edens, thinning out its ranks, capturing its females in order to organize slavery from the very maternal womb, imposing their will upon the powerless race of the vanquished and through humiliation forced them into breaking the admittingly superior but destructive link of language with their enemy, and as the last hope for survival taking refuge in the night of animality.

And what horrors, what enormous brutality did the conquerors not commit with this semi-beast during the evolutionary process, so that after having tasted intellectual rapture which is the heavenly fruit of the bibles, he would resign himself to the surrender of his stock in the degrading equality of an inferior race; to the retrogression that crystallized his intelligence forever into the automated gestures of an acrobat; to this great cowardice of life which would make, as an emblematic beast, the back of a conquered subject stoop, stamping it with that doleful embarrassment that permeates his derisory figure.

This is what had at the very doorstep of success aroused my bad mood in the depth of the atavistic limbo. Over the span of a million years, the word, with its spell, stirred up the ancient simian soul: but in the way of that temptation which was to lift the clouds of darkness which sheltered their animality, stood the ancestral memory, disseminated among their species by an instinctive horror, piled up age upon age like a huge wall.

Yzur in the very throes of death did not loose consciousness. With eyes closed, feeble breathing, uneven pulse and absolute calm, he experienced a peaceful agony, interrupted only on occasions when he would turn his sad face, which resembled that of an old man, toward me with a heartbreaking expression of eternity. And the last afternoon, the afternoon of his death, was when the most extraordinary thing occurred which motivated me to write this story.

I had dozed a bit at his bedside, overcome by the heat and silence of emerging twilight, when suddenly I felt someone pulling at my wrist.

I woke up startled. The monkey with his eyes fully opened, was definitely dying that time, and his expression was so human, that it

que me infundió horror; pero su mano, sus ojos, me atraían con tanta elocuencia hacia él, que tuve que inclinarme inmediato a su rostro; y entonces, con su último suspiro, el último suspiro que coronaba y desvanecía a la vez mi esperanza, brotaron –estoy seguro– brotaron en un murmullo (¿Cómo explicar el tono de una voz que ha permanecido sin hablar diez mil siglos?) estas palabras cuya humanidad reconciliaba las especies:

–AMO, AGUA. AMO, MI AMO...

❖

filled me with terror; but his hand, his eyes, were so eloquently drawing me toward him, that I had to lean my face next to his; and then, with his last breath, a breath which was alternately fulfilling and dispelling my hope, came forth, –I am certain– came forth ever so softly (how do you describe the tone of a voice that has remained silent for ten thousand centuries?) these words whose humanity had once again reconciled the species:

"MASTER, WATER. MASTER, MY MASTER..."

❖

VOCABULARY

acertar a. To manage (to do something), to be successful (at doing something). Sᴜɴ. *Dar con, atinar.*

acometer. Undertake, start on, begin. Sᴜɴ. *Tentar, comenzar.*

acorde con. Consistant with, in keeping with. Sᴜɴ. *De acuerdo con, conforme a.*

acuerdo. *Ponerse de acuerdo.* Como to an understanding. To assent, to agree on. Sᴜɴ. *Coincidir en., consentir.*

acurrucado. Bending, crouching, squatting. Sᴜɴ. *Agachado, inclinado.*

adelante. *En adelante.* From this moment on, from now on. Sᴜɴ. *De ahora en adelante, a partir de ahora.*

ademán. Gesture. Sᴜɴ. *Gesto, movimiento.*

además de. Besides, in addition to. Sᴜɴ. *Aparte de, fuera de.*

adherido. Glued, fasten on, attached. Sᴜɴ. *Pegado, fijado.*

formar (plan). Draw up, formulate, draft. Sᴜɴ. *Confeccionar, formular.*

advertencia. Admonition, warning. Sᴜɴ. *Aviso.*

agolparse. Flock, swarm. Sᴜɴ. *Acumularse, amontonarse.*

agotar. Exhaust, deplete, drain, use up. Sᴜɴ. *Consumir, gastar, terminar.*

aisladamente. Separately. Apart. Sᴜɴ. *Por separado.*

algarabía. Racket, noise, tumult. Sᴜɴ. *Alboroto, bulla.*

alzar. To lift, raise. Sᴜɴ. *Levantar, izar, subir.*

ambicionar. Go for, strive for. Sᴜɴ. *Anhelar, ansiar, desear vivamente.*

anómala. Irregular, abnormal. Sᴜɴ. *Insólito.*

ansia. Yearning, longing, craving. Sᴜɴ. *Anhelo, deseo, afán.*

ante. Before, in front of. Sᴜɴ. *Delante de.*

apelar. Resort to, call upon, appeal to. Sᴜɴ. *Acudir a, recurrir a.*

apenas. As soon as. Sᴜɴ. *Tan pronto como.*

apetecer. Long for, yearn for, look forward to. Sᴜɴ. *Ansiar, anhelar.*

apoderarse. Get hold of, seize. Sᴜɴ. *Adueñarse.*

apreciar. To value, prize. Sᴜɴ. *Estimar, valorar.*

aprovecharse de. Benefit (by), profit from, take advantage of. Sᴜɴ. *Beneficiar, sacar ventaja, sacar provecho.*

apto. Capable, quick to learn. *Sin. Capaz, perito.*

arrancar. Grab, tear away, snatch away. Sᴜɴ. *Quitar, arrebatar.*

arrollar. Roll up, coil up, wind up. Sᴜɴ. *Enrollar, envolver, ovillar.*

asaz. Rather. Sᴜɴ. *Bastante, muy.*

asentarse. (bird) to alight; (liquid)

to settle; (arquit.) to settle, sink, subside; (fig) to settle, establish oneself.

asentir. Agree, go along with. Sin. *Estar de acuerdo, coincidir.*

asomarse a. To appear, come into sight, emerge, show up. Sin. *Surgir, presentarse.*

aterrar. Terrify, strike terror into. Sin. *Atemorizar, espantar.*

atinar. Guess, solve, find the solution for. Sin. *Adivinar, acertar.*

audaz. Daring, bold, audacious. Sin. *Atrevido, temerario.*

avenirse. Conform, harmonize, agree with. Sin. *Amoldarse, conformarse.*

azorado. Confounded, perturbed. Sin. *Aturdido, abrumado.*

bambolear. Roll, sway, rock. Sin. *Mecerse, balancearse.*

barullo. Row, uproar, din. Sin. *Ajetreo, trajín.*

bicho. Small animal, insect. *Ser un bicho raro.* To be an odd person.

botar. (Latin America). To throw, hurl. Sin. *Echar, arrojar, tirar.*

bruces. *De bruces.* To lie face downward, to lie flat on one's stomach. Sin. *Boca abajo.*

burlón. Mocking, derisive, sarcastic. Sin. *Cínico, irónico. mordaz.*

cazar. *Cazar a tiros.* To hunt down with a rifle.

ceder. Cease, come to an end. Sin. *Terminar.*

certidumbre. Certainty, conviction. Sin. *Certeza, seguridad.*

chasco. Disappointment. Sin. *Desengaño.*

chile. (Latin America). Lies. Sin. *Mentira.*

claudicar. To give up. *Darse por vencido.*

colocar. Put, place. Sin. *Poner.*

competencia. Competence, expertise, professional skill. Sin. *Abilidad, pericia.*

complacerse en. Take pleasure in, relish, delight in, enjoy. Sin. *Gozar, disfrutar de, deleitarse en.*

componer. *Componerse (el tiempo).* To clear up (weather). Sin. *Despejarse.*

concerniente. Regarding, with respect to. Sin. *Acerca de, en cuanto a.*

conjunto. Whole, totality. Sin. *Totalidad.*

conmovido. Moved, touched, stirred. Sin. *Emocionado. enternecido.*

consistente en. Made up of, consisting of. Sin. *Compuesto de.*

contar con. Count on, depend on, rely on. Sin. *Confiar en, fiarse de.*

contornos. Surroundings, vicinity, neighborhood. Sin. *Alrededores, inmediaciones.*

conveniente. Advisable, wise. Sin. *Aconsejable, deseable.*

convertirse. Become, develop (into), turn (into). Sin. *Llegar a ser.*

corazonada. Feeling, hunch. Sin. *Presagio, presentimiento.*

corregir. To amend, correct, rectify, set right. Sin. *Rectificar.*

cosquilla. *Hacer cosquillas.* To tickle.

costar. Require, demand, need. Sin. *Necesitar, precisar, requerir.*

criatura. Small child.

cuando. *Cuando más.* At most. Sin. *A lo sumo.*

cumplir. Accomplish, achieve, fullfil, carry out, implement. SIN. *Realizar, llevar a cabo.*

decir. *Está de más decir que.* It goes without saying that.

deglución. Swallowing. SIN. *Injestión.*

dejarse + infinitive. To let oneself be + past participle. *Dejarse agarrar.* To let oneself be caught, grabbed, taken.

delantera. *Tomar la delantera.* To take the lead.

descoyuntarse. To dislocate, put out of joint. SIN. *Descomponerse.*

desenvolver. Unwind, uncoil. SIN. *Desenrrollar, desplegar.*

desesperar. Become desperate, despair, give up. SIN. *Perder la esperanza.*

destellar. Sparkle, shine, radiate. SIN. *Brillar, relucir, resplandecer.*

destronar. Dethrone, depose, remove. SIN. *Deponer, destituir.*

desvanece. Efface, erase, wipe out. SIN. *Borrar.*

desvanecido. Giddy, dizzy. SIN. *Mareado.*

detenido. Held back, detained, checked. SIN. *Parado, arrestado.*

difunto. Dead person, deceased. SIN. *Fallecido, muerto.*

disgustarse. To be annoyed, get upset, feel offended. SIN. *Enfadarse, amoscarse.*

disimuladamente. Furtively, secretly, covertly. SIN. *En secreto, furtivamente, a escondidas, a hurtadillas.*

disimulo. Craftiness, cunning, cleverness. SIN. *Astucia, sutileza.*

disparatado. Foolish, nonsensical, absurd. SIN. *Insensato, absurdo.*

dominio. Power, sway, authority. SIN. *Autoridad, poder.*

dubitativo. Hesitant, uncertain, doubtful. SIN. *Perplejo, vacilante, dudoso.*

ejercer. Hold, perform, practice. *Sin. Desempeñar.*

encajarse. To become jammed, stuck. Sin. *Atrancarse, atascarse.*

encolerizar. Anger, annoy, irritate. *Sin. Enojar, enfadar.*

encresparse. (feathers) to ruffle; (hair) to curl. (fig.) to anger, irritate

endiablado. Devilish, fiendish. SIN. *Endemoniado.*

engatuzar. To coach, wheedle, soaf-soap. SIN. *Engañar.*

esparcir. To scatter, disperse, sprinkle. SIN. *Salpicar, sembrar.*

establecido. Accepted, established. SIN. *Cierto, consagrado.*

estirpe. Lineage, stock, race. SIN. *Casta, linaje, alcurnia.*

estorbar. Hamper, hinder, impede. SIN. *Dificultar, entorpecer, obstaculizar.*

estrafalario. Bizarre, strange, odd. SIN. *Extraño, curioso.*

estrecharse. To get narrower, or tighter. SIN. *Reducirse, angostarse.*

estribar. To lie in, rest in. SIN. *Estar en.*

faenas. Affairs, business, matters. SIN. *Asuntos, quehaceres.*

fallar. Fail, falter, stall. SIN. *Fracasar, malograrse.*

falta. *Sin falta.* Without fail, definitely. SIN. *Con toda seguriad.*

faltar. Be lacking, be missing.

felizmente. Fortunately, happily. SIN. *Afortunadamente, por suerte.*

fijarse. Fix on, focus on, notice, pay attention. Sɪɴ. *Fijarse en, reconcentrarse en.*

fogata. Fire, campfire. Sɪɴ. *Hogar, hoguera, lumbre.*

fondo. *En el fondo*. Actually, in reality, as a matter of fact. Sɪɴ. *En realidad, en verdad.*

forma. *En forma tal*. In such a way.

forzar. Enforce, oblige, compel. Sɪɴ. *Imponer, obligar.*

fracaso. Failure, flop, miscarriage. Sɪɴ. *Fallo, fiasco.*

francachela. Binge, carousal, spree (drinking). Sɪɴ. *Bacanal, juerga.*

fulgurar. Glitter, glow, shine. Sɪɴ. *Brillar, destellar.*

ganas. *Tener ganas*. To feel like, long for, to be in the mood for. Sɪɴ. *Apetecer, anhelar, desear.*

gimotear. Groan, moan. Sɪɴ. *Gemir.*

golpe. *De golpe*. Suddenly, unexpectedly. Sɪɴ. *De repente.*

grabado. Engraved, etched. Sɪɴ, *Tallado, recortado.*

hacer. *Por lo que hace*. In regard to, concerning. Sɪɴ. *En cuanto a.*

harto. *Tener (estar) harto*. To have one's fill of. To be disgusted. Sɪɴ. *Estar disgustado.*

herir (poetic). To touch, caress. Sɪɴ. *Acariciar, tocar.*

ignorar. To be unaware of, be ignorant of. Sɪɴ. *Desconocer, no estar enterado de.*

imperio. Dominion, control, power. Sɪɴ. *Poder.*

incitar a. Instigate, spur on, prod, urge. Sɪɴ. *Instigar.*

infausto. Disastrous, calamitous, catastrophic. Sɪɴ. *Funesto, nefasto,* *desastroso, catastrófico.*

infinidad de. A great many, a large number of. Sɪɴ. *Muchísimos, un montón de.*

infructuosa. Unsuccessful, fruitless. Sɪɴ. *Inútil.*

insigne. Noted, celebrated, famous. Sɪɴ. *Afamado, célebre, conocido.*

intervenir. Intervene, take part in. Sɪɴ. *Participar, tomar parte.*

juzgar. *A juzgar por*. Judging by.

langosta. (1) Locust, (2) lobster.

lanzarse. Charge at, make a rush at, make for, run towards. Sɪɴ. *Abalanzarse sobre, precipitarse sobre.*

llegar a. Succeed, achieve, attain. Sɪɴ. *Alcanzar, conseguir, lograr, obtener.*

llevar (time). Take. Sɪɴ. *tardar.*

locura. *Tener locura por*. To be crazy about, to like very much.

macizo. Compact, dense, solid. Sɪɴ. *Sólido, compacto.*

madriguera. Burrow, den, lair. Sɪɴ. *Cubil, guarida.*

medio. (1) *En medio de*. In the midst of, amid, among, between. Sɪɴ. *Entre.* (2) *Por medio de*. By means of.

morado. Purple, violet. Sɪɴ. *Púrpura, violeta.*

necedad. Foolishness, stupidity. Sɪɴ. *Estupidez, torpeza.*

notable. Outstanding, extraordinary, noteworthy, remarkable. Sɪɴ. *Extraordinario, saliente.*

obsequio. Present, gift. Sɪɴ. Regalo.

ocultar. Hide, conceal. Sɪɴ. *Esconder.*

padecer. Suffer from. Sɪɴ. *Sufrir de.*

parte. *Por otra parte*. On the other hand.

partir. Leave. SIN. *Salir.*

patojo (Central America). Boy, lad. SIN. *Chico, muchacho.*

pelado. (head, etc.) shorn, hairless; (bark of a tree, etc.) bare, smooth; (bone) clean; (apple) peeled; (field, etc.) treeless, bare; (landscape) bare.

pendejada (Latin America). Foolishness, stupidity. SIN. *Tontería, estupidez.*

perseguir. Chase, pursue, go after. SIN. *Andar tras.*

plañidero. Lamenting, plaintive. SIN. *Quejumbroso, lamentoso.*

plegar. Wrinkle. SIN. *Arrugar.*

poco. *A poco.* Soon. SIN. *Dentro de poco.*

porfiado. Persistent, stubborn. SIN. *Tenaz, persistente.*

postulado. Assumption, hypothesis. SIN. *Axioma, supuesto.*

postura. Attitude, conduct, manner. SIN. *Actitud, aire.*

predominar. To be prevalent. SIN. *Prevalecer.*

prender. Affix, attach, fasten. SIN. *Sujetar.*

presentir. To anticipate, foresee, expect. SIN. *Anticipar, prever, adivinar.*

producir. Create, originate, produce. SIN. *Crear, general, originar.*

provenir. Come from, arise from. SIN. *Venir de, proceder de.*

provisto de. Supplied with, possessing, endowed with. SIN. *Dotado.*

provocar. Bring about, cause, create. SIN. *Ocasionar, producir.*

puntapie. Boot, kick. SIN. *Patada.*

quebrar. Go bankrupt, bust, fail. SIN. *Hacer quiebra, hacer bancarrota.*

rabón. Without a tail. SIN. *Sin rabo.*

raciocinio. Reasoning, train of thought. SIN. *Pensamiento, razonamiento.*

reclamar. Demand, exact, claim. SIN. *Exigir, demandar.*

recoger. Collect, accumulate, amass, compile, gather. SIN. *Acumular, amontonar.*

recorrer. Roam, travel around, go from one place to the next. SIN. *Andar sin rumbo, deambular.*

reducido. Limited, restricted to. Sin. *Limitado, restringido.*

referir. Narrate, recount, relate, tell. SIN. *Contar, narrar, relatar.*

remate. Close out, auction sale.

remediar. Remedy, fix, cure. SIN. *Sanar, curar, arreglar.*

responder. Reply. SIN. *Contestar.*

restante. *En lo restante.* As to the rest. SIN. *En cuanto a lo demás.*

resultar. End up, wind up, result in. SIN. *Acabar, finalizar, terminar.*

retener. Halt, stop. SIN. *Parar, atajar.*

retornar. Return. SIN. *Volver.*

romper con (una persona). Break off (with a person). SIN. *Cortar, interrumpir.*

rozar. Brush, graze, rub against. SIN. *Rasar, pasar por.*

sahumar. To perfume (with incense). SIN. *Aromatizar, perfumar, incensar.*

seguro. *A buen seguro.* Certainly, surely, beyond question. SIN. *Seguramente, sin duda alguna.*

semejante. Similar, like. SIN. *Parecido, similar.*

señalar. To point to. SIN. *Indicar, mostrar.*

soltar. Drop, let fall, let go, release. SIN. *Dejar caer.*

sonseras. Foolishness, stupidity. SIN. *Disparate, desatino, tontería.*

sostener. Carry, support, hold up. SIN. *Soportar, sustentar.*

sublevarse. Rebel, revolt. SIN. *Rebelarse, alzarse.*

suceder. Happen, befall. SIN. *Producirse, pasar.*

suelto. *Andar suelto.* To be on the loose, go unhampered.

suerte. *Por suerte.* Fortunately, luckily. SIN. *Afortunadamente.*

sujeto. Subject, theme, topic. SIN. *Asunto, tema.*

surgir. Appear, show up, emerge. SIN. *Aparecer, emerger.*

suya. *Quedarse con la suya.* To have one's own way.

tanto... como. As well as.

tender. Lean to (towards), tend (to, towards), have a tendency (to). SIN. *Tener tendencia a, inclinarse a.*

tendido. Extended, stretched, outstretched. SIN. *Estirado.*

tentar. Test, try out, undertake. SIN. *Experimentar, atentar.*

tentativa. Attempt, effort, endeavor, try. SIN. *Esfuerzo, intento.*

ténue. Faint, slim, slender. SIN. *Delgado, fino.*

tesón. Persistence, insistence, tenacity, firmness. SIN. *Tenacidad, perseverencia.*

tinieblas. Dark, darkness, gloom, obscurity. SIN. *Oscuridad, penumbra.*

ton. *Sin ton ni son.* Without rhyme or reason.

trance. *En trance de.* In the process of. On the point of.

tranco. Stride, pace, step. SIN. *Pisada, zancada, paso.*

tras. After. SIN. *Después.*

traspasar. Traverse, cross. SIN. *Cruzar, atravesar.*

tratar a. Associate with, mingle with. SIN. *Frecuentar, tener trato con.*

tratarse de. To involve, have to do with, concern, pertain to. SIN. *Tener que ver con.*

trepar. Ascend, climb, mount. SIN. *Escalar, subir.*

triturar. Smash, crush, squash. SIN. *Aplastar, destrozar.*

tropezar con. Stumble, take a false step, trip. SIN. *Dar un traspie.*

tumbar. Knock down. SIN. *Derribar, hacer caer.*

turbado. Distressed, dismayed. SIN. *Desconcertado, alarmado.*

velozmente. Rapidly, hastily. SIN. *Rápidamente, de prisa.*

vencido. *Darse por vencido.* To give up.

vigorizarse. Strenghten, grow stronger. SIN. *Fortalecer, reforzar.*

vincular. Link, bind, tie. SIN. *Atar, ligar, unir.*

zarpar. Sail, leave port, weigh anchor. SIN. *Levanta anclas, salir (buque).*

zumbar. Buzz, drone, hum. SIN. *Bordonear, rehilar.*

ORDER FORM

 BILINGUAL BOOK PRESS
Quality Bilingual Publications

BILINGUAL BOOK PRESS
10977 Santa Monica Blvd.
Los Angeles, CA 90025

Date _____

Order # _____

COPIES	DESCRIPTION	ISBN	PRICE	TOTAL
	Bilingual Dictionary of Mexican Spanish	1-886835-01-2	$19.95	
	The Best of Latin American Short Stories	1-886835-02-0	$10.95	
	Bilingual Dictionary of Latin American Spanish	1-886835-03-9	$19.95	
	Two Holiday Folktales from Mexico	1-886835-04-7	$10.00	
	Message:			

SUBTOTAL	
CALIFORNIA STATE TAX (8.25%)	
SUBTOTAL	
SHIPPING & HANDLING (8%. $3.00 min.)	
TOTAL	

SEND TO

Name: _____

Address: _____

City: _____ State _____ Zip _____

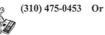 **(310) 475-0453 Or**   **Fax (310) 473-6132**